For Emma, you are my heartbeat.

Prologue

The window hummed open just enough to flick out the match and let cigarette smoke escape.

"Jesus Christ, Maxi, do you have to?"

"Yep. Especially with your driving. Be grateful I opened the window."

"It's my car."

"So?" He blew smoke at the windscreen and watched it disperse around the car.

Butch pouted. "I'm not afraid of you."

He smiled and blew smoke out the window

"You're such a whiny arsehole. I open the window and I put out the smokes in my ashtray."

"It makes my car stink."

"So do your protein farts. For a muscleman you're such a wimp."

They travelled on in silence for a while, the only view the dark road, lit up by their headlights.

"Are we killing this bloke tonight?"

"If he deserves it. I'll decide when we talk to him. Just follow my lead."

Chapter 1

Captain Nightingale tried to look out the window into the dark evening but, from his desk, all he could see was the reflection of his study. "I need inspiration from the sea, Daisy", he said to his little dog. Daisy looked up and cocked her head, when he got up and opened the window, and then went back to licking her stuffed toy pig when she realised no food or walk was being offered. After staring out at the horizon that glowed with a distant faded light, the Captain went back to his desk and fed a sheet of paper in his typewriter and started on his speech for the new season of pleasure cruises around the bay.

Welcome onboard the Mustang Rose, named after my late wife's passions; vintage sports cars and roses.

[wait for reaction]

Before we shove off we'll get the boring safety messages over with and then head out of the harbour and along the coast to discover the smuggler's cave and seabird nests. On the way out I will talk about the history of Rosegarden and how it came to be the way it is now. On the way back you'll be able to see the village in all her beauty. A view you don't get in the village itself of course.

[safety announcement]

[refreshment announcement]

Ladies and gentlemen, as we set out let me tell you about a young man called Guy Lambert who came back from the First World War a highly decorated officer. With his father's blessing he set out to travel and see what the rest of the world had to offer. The more he travelled the more he began to believe that his own family's wealth was very much like that of, what was then called, the empire. It had been acquired, and was mainly based on, the exploitation of others. His father passed away shortly before his return, almost two years later. He was the sole heir to the estate and farmland to the north and the beach and fisherman's village to the south. He sold the farms off to the families that had worked them for generations and gave them financial freedom so long as the farms remained working farms and were not sold off to developers.

The fishing village was already abandoned by this stage and the first thing to happen was the three fisherman's cottages were refurbished and turned in to the Fisherman's Arms which still serves delicious food and drinks today. There was a small pub at the other end of the village called the Crow's Nest. This is still there but is now a wine bar for those with a more upmarket pallet.

[allow for laughter]

The biggest change, by far, was designed by Guy Lambert and a group of like-minded architects. They believed in a more egalitarian and liberal society. They set about demolishing the old manor house. The only thing they kept was the old rose garden, which, of course, gave the village its name and the central section of the old lawn which serves as the town square green. The layout of the town will be described when we head back and you get a great view of the village.

But it wasn't just the buildings that were new. The population was too. Guy Lambert set about populating the village with people from all over the world and a few from this country too. Of course, in time, all the residents were from this country. The first family to settle was the Martini family. Alfonse Martini saved Guy Lambert's life in Italy and both then stayed at the military hospital that also attended the famous author Ernest Hemingway. Whether they met him or not, who knows. It's nice to think that they all got blotto together.

[possible laughter]

The next people to become citizens of the village were the people who helped build it. These were also people from all over the world and this country too. The only qualification you needed to stay was respect for others and a kind heart and open mind. More will be said about the history and philosophy of the village on the way back in, but, for now, please sit and relax and enjoy the views and enjoy a drink from the bar which is now open.

[Pause}

Ladies and gentlemen we have now left the harbour and will go a little distance along the coast. What you will notice at first is nothing. That's right, nothing. Smugglers used the caves because they can only be seen from certain angles. Keep looking at the area with the rock formation in front of it and, in a little while, you'll see a gang of ne'er do wells; smuggling rum no doubt.
There they are.

[Make sure usuals are willing to portray smugglers]

We'll cut the engines and just drift here a while for photo opportunities.

[Ask Danny about social media things]

[Seabird section. Speak to Hattie to see if she'll get involved]

OK. Now for the best view of Rosegarden that you'll ever see.

As we come back in to the bay the first thing you'll notice is the splendid headdress worn by our lovely village and where she gets her name. The effect is kept all year. When the real roses die we have a day when everyone plants a ceramic rose in a pattern designed by our resident artist Ross Roberts. As I previously told you, rose park is the oldest remaining part of the estate. The Lambert family's stately home and its grounds were all demolished by the first Guy Lambert in the early 1920s to make way for a village designed by him and like minded architects.
How many of you have visited Rose Park?

[pause for murmurs and possible lecture by tourists]

It does have many blind paths and secret lovers benches that are well signposted and not secret at all.

[pause for laughter]

As you look at the village, imagine you're on a stage looking at an empty theatre. The houses are arranged so that everyone has a view of the sea. The houses get larger the further away from the sea (or stage) you are, until, at the top, you have two large houses. The Royal boxes of the village, if you will. On the left is the house of the current Guy Lambert, grandson of the founder of Rosegarden. He is landlord and mayor of everyone. But the rent is very cheap and businesses share their profits for cheap rates too and he is a well liked chap. The other Royal box is the home and studio of Guy Lambert's second cousin Ross Roberts. The same chap who designs the ceramic rose patterns.
The original Guy Lambert was an egalitarian and so the houses with better access to the sea are the smaller, cheaper ones. Live in a big house and you'll have to walk up the hill after your seafront promenade.

[pause]

Captain Nightingale glanced over at Daisy. "I'll read it to you when it's done, old girl." Daisy raised her head then lowered it, getting ready to be lulled to sleep by the tapping of the typewriter keys.

He read what he had written and made a mental note of changes to make and then continued.

The neat rows of houses that cascade down the hill were all built in a space of three years. The workforce were the first residents of the village (if they wished to stay) and many of their offspring live here today. As you walk around the village you'll probably notice how varied the population is. The first Guy Lambert came back from the First World War and travelled for a couple of years all over what was called the Empire. He realised that the family's estate, like the old Empire, was built on and thrived from the exploitation of others.

[say this again to make the point?]

It was then he decided to create an idyllic village to be enjoyed equally by people from all over the world. You will see, below Guy Lambert's house, is a beautiful white building with a copper roof. The House of Worship. On the outside walls of the building you will see the symbols of every religion in the world. Anyone and everyone can worship in whatever way they wish or just sit and reflect. Some of you may know that our village motto is 'Equality and Respect For All'.

On the other side of the village, below Ross Roberts house is where my wife worshipped - May's Garage, run by Emma May.

[pause for possible laughter]

Emma is now the proud owner of my late wife's Mustang.

In the middle of the village, both physically and metaphorically, is the town square. This was once the estate's grand lawn. The green in the middle is what is left of the lawn. On the east (or right as we look at it) is a museum, gallery and library in that beautiful art deco building which is mirrored on the west by the civic offices.

Further down the hill are the rows of shops and world cuisine restaurants. For a lovely afternoon tea you'll be wise to go to Maggie's, far to the left of the magnificent Seaview Hotel.

A splendid example of art deco architecture, the hotel was regularly visited by Hollywood actors of yesteryear and television crews of today and is loved by everyone who visits Rosegarden and anyone who has seen the various period dramas filmed there.

To the right of the hotel is home to the best fish and chips this side of John O'Groats. The Gutty Shark.

[wait for chuckling to subside]

On either side of the beach are our two pubs. For a traditional pub experience with good hearty pub fare, The Fisherman's Arms fits the bill.

On the other side of the beach is the Crow's Nest. More of a bistro or wine bar, if that's your thing, but the oldest pub in the area.

And that brings us to our beautiful award winning beach. Clean and safe for swimming. Oh and, of course, what beach would be complete without an ice cream van.

At that moment a strange electronic drone that sounded like 'Donna e Mobile' disturbed the still night and then faded away in a sudden, exhausted last note.

Daisy started barking.

"What on earth?" Captain Nightingale got up and tried to look toward Rosegarden but saw only darkness.

"Alright, Daisy old girl. Calm down now."

Daisy looked up at him, gave a half hearted final bark and went back to sleep.

Later that night, a car drove past on the only road in to Rosegarden and drove back out a few hours later. Must have been a farmer going to the Fisherman's.

Chapter 2

Between the edge of the beach and Captain Nightingale's cottage and dock, at Lookout Point, is a mile of sand dunes regularly visited by bird watchers, lovers and those trying to hide from something or someone. Dean had been there many times, birdwatching by day and star gazing at night. He sometimes used it as a hiding place from the world at large there but never as a lover's retreat. That is until that evening.

"It's a really lovely evening." , he said, "Look at the moon, it's beautiful."

Pearl finished gnawing all the meat from the chicken drumstick and threw the bone over the dune and onto the road.

"A fox or something will have that." She said to no one in particular then turned to Dean sucking the grease and juices from her fingers.

"You what?" She asked between finger cleaning.

"The moon is beautiful."

She glanced over the sea.

"Yeah. I guess."

In all her twenty years living in Rosegarden she had never been to the sand dunes. She had sometimes parked in the car park next to them with a boy and sometimes with her sister after a disco night in the Bosun's Locker, five miles west along the sea road.

She reached in to his picnic cooler bag and extracted the last drumstick which she stripped clean in less than a minute.

Dean tried again.

"You can tell Easter is next weekend because the moon is nearly full. It's the first full moon after Spring Equinox."

Pearl sucked and licked the chicken drumstick and threw the bone over the dune to join all the others she had thrown.

"A crab or something will have that." She said to no one in particular then turned to Dean sucking the grease and juices from her fingers.

"Easter. The moon. What are you going on about? Any dessert in that bag? I couldn't feel any."

Dean produced a two pack of chocolate donuts from his satchel and handed them over to her.

"Not being funny but you come out with some random boring stuff."

Dean turned away and looked at the sea and wanted to be alone with his surroundings and the sky.

"You're really good looking though."

"Thanks." He said and was about to say more when the sound of an ice cream van's chimes blared out two lines of 'Donna E Mobile" then dwindled in to a slow low pitched groan like a deflated opera singer. Silence followed for a few seconds and then came the sound of tyres on tarmac followed by a metallic bump. Shouts and running footsteps disappeared in to the night.

"The fuck was that?" Pearl asked with a mouth full of donut.

"Sounded like an ice cream van gone wrong."

"Oh well. Never mind that, or the moon or Easter, I'm all yours, lover boy."

Dean turned around to see Pearl with arms akimbo and a chicken greasy, chocolate smudged puckered mouth.

"I'd better go and investigate." he said.

Chapter 3

Captain Nightingale stepped out of his thatched cottage attired in what he called his Picasso outfit of red striped crew neck shirt, cream sweater over his shoulders, khaki shorts and sandals, with the non-Picasso additions of calf length white socks, and a plain blue baseball cap.

After a huge intake of fresh, early April morning air, he declared it to be a good start to a good day and, as it was Monday, to a good week. After a quick check for traffic he strode forward to his dock to check on The Mustang Rose.

"Come on, Daisy. Keep up."

Daisy squatted to pee and mark her territory then trotted next to him with a happy wagging tail.

The Mustang Rose passed as shipshape, they went back to the road to Rosegarden. His stride was somewhere between a walk and a march and with each step he looked about to make sure that everything was in its place. He had walked this route every morning for the last seventeen years and he knew what should be where and what shouldn't be anywhere.

Daisy's nose was going crazy and she zigzagged here and there, backwards and forwards. "What can you smell old girl? Better get to it before you do. He looked ahead and spotted the chicken bones near the dunes. Daisy was still trying to find the smell when he picked them up.

"Hm. People leaving litter around and hoping foxes will have it I suppose" he said to Daisy as he gathered up the bones and put them in an empty poo bag. Daisy quickly got over her disappointment in missing out on a snack and zigzagged her way towards the village leaving her scent where necessary.

They walked a little further and the Captain looked over towards the car park.

"What the devil!" He said loudly, walking down the slope of the car park toward an ice cream van that had no right being parked at that weird angle. It was Frankie Flake's. He didn't know the man's real name. Everyone called him Frankie Flake.

Marching towards it he noticed cigarette butts in a pile in the middle of the car park and beer bottles on the far side.

"Damn yobs!

"Try not to pee on anything, Daisy" he shouted back. She wagged her tail then peed at the top of the slope. The Captain watched as it flowed downwards. "Oh well."

The ice cream van appeared to have only stopped reversing because the lamp post was in the way. The door was open on the drivers side. It wasn't your regular ice cream van. It was a converted Luton van with the tail lift and shutter door replaced by a panel welcoming everyone to Rosegarden.

The Captain looked inside the driver's cabin. A bowie knife lay on the floor between the driver and passenger seats. The keys were still in the ignition and a glasses case lay in the passenger's footwell. He decided not to touch anything just in case a crime had been committed; like stealing an ice cream van.

Walking around the outside of the van, nothing seemed out of order, apart from a small dent in the back. The ordering hatch was closed. He tried to look inside. There was the very sweet smell of vanilla ice cream and something else he couldn't put his finger on.

Back in the cab he noticed the lock on the door, between the cab and the serving area, had been tampered with. Possibly with the Bowie knife. Nothing happened when he gave the door a push. He shook his head when he noticed that the door opened by pulling. He got his fingers around a part of the door and pulled.

There, in front of him, laying face down in melted ice cream mixed with blood, was Frankie Flake.

Chapter 4

Even though Danny Fisher was a man now, most of the villagers seemed to still see him as the grocery boy. But then it had taken three years for people to stop calling him Jimmy. The previous four delivery boys were all called Jimmy. Some people seemed outraged that Bill Fisher, the grocer, had hired a boy whose name wasn't Jimmy. Bill had to remind them that this latest recruit was, in fact, his son and that he wasn't going to change his name now. Danny's mother wouldn't stand for it. That was ten years ago and he hadn't progressed further than bicycle deliveries. His dad did the van deliveries outside Rosegarden to the nearby farms and the Bosun's Locker publican. The town gossips said that Bill was given all the beer and grub he could manage at the pub and groceries weren't the only things he delivered to the farmers' wives while the farmers were out in the fields.

Danny didn't think there was any truth in the tittle tattle but it would explain why he was stuck to bicycle deliveries and helping his mum out in the shop. It was so frustrating though. He wanted his own shop. A computer and smart phone shop where he offered repairs and technical help. There was a gap in the market in the area. He could make a good living from it and in turn so would Rosegarden. He had to put it to the committee. His dad wouldn't. He thought the idea was stupid and not for Rosegarden. His girlfriend, Peggy, said that her uncle, Tony Martini, was interested in helping him out. But he wasn't on the committee again for another two months after Mama Cassandra had her turn as restaurant representative. Hopefully Tony could persuade Guy Lambert outside of the committee meeting. In the meantime it's coke, toilet rolls and spuds to the Captain's house. There, right on cue stood the Captain waving his arms. "Danny! Stop!"

"Morning, Captain. Hello Daisy!"

Daisy wagged her tail and got on her hind legs to get closer to him and rested her front paws on his thighs.

"Morning, Danny. Look, come over here quickly! Have you got one of those computer phones that can take photos?"

Danny suppressed a laugh. "A smartphone? Yeah. I've got an iPhone."

"Good. Good. No need to brag though. Come quickly. No. Tell you what, deliver that stuff toot sweet and then come back here. Leave it in the usual place but hurry back!"

"What's the matter?"

"I'll explain when you get back."

He watched Danny wobble his start and then cycle quickly to the cottage. He returned in five minutes.

"Alright. Down here. Come now."

"What's Frankie Flake's van doing down there?"

"Exactly. I need you to take several photographs as evidence just in case someone fools around with, erm, well, you'll see."

Danny got off his bike and got out his phone.

"Right. Firstly take photos of the general area. Include those cigarette butts in the middle. Then those beer bottles over there."

Danny did as the Captain said and showed him the photos on his phone.

"Excellent! Right, now the ice cream van from here. Then all around the van."

"Shouldn't we tell Frankie or Tony about all this?"

"Ah, yes, good point. I'll get to that in a moment. Just carry on."

Danny was mystified but it was exciting and something different to the usual. He took the photos.

"I can video all this if you like."

"Can you?" The Captain was amazed. "Alright. Everything you have already photographed, now video."

Danny videoed it all turning his phone on its side so it would look like a proper video camera. The Captain stayed behind him so as not to get in the way. Daisy wasn't as bothered and wandered in and out of shot.

"Alright, Danny. The next bit is a little, erm, messy let's say. But be calm. You need to keep taking photos and video. Let's go in to the cabin and photograph the dashboard and floor. You'll see."

It was still exciting to Danny but now there seemed to be something else. Where was Frankie Flake?

"First off, photo the keys in the ignition, then the knife on the floor and then the scratched keyhole area."

Danny snapped and videoed as requested.

"Now, Danny, you need to brace yourself for the next bit. I'm going to open this door and you will see a dead body. I believe it to be Frankie Flake. Just think of him as asleep. Face down. In ice cream. Ice cream mixed with blood."

Danny stared at him for a moment. "What flavour?"

"What? What do you mean what bloody flavour! What does it matter? If it helps it looks like a combination of raspberry ripple and strawberry, but that's the blood. What flavour, indeed!"

The Captain opened the door to reveal Frankie Flake as he had found him before but now there seemed to be more ice cream on the floor.

"Shit!

What?

No!

Oh Christ.

I've never seen a dead body before." His face was contorted in horror and disbelief.

"The ice cream in the freezer is melting even more now and there seems to be a leak somewhere." He looked around at Danny who was trying to look away but couldn't.

"I feel sick."

"Well, make sure you get some good photos first."

Danny snapped all he could without going in to the serving area then went outside for air.

"Good work, Danny. Now, Daisy can sit in your front basket and you can dubby me in to the village."

"What? Shouldn't we phone the police?"

"Not until the council agree to it. Now, best foot forward, get me to the council meeting. It should be starting around now. Let's just hope nobody tampers with Frankie. Right, where's Daisy now?"

They walked around and found her licking the puddle of ice cream that had dripped from the back of the van.

"Let's hope that's not evidence, eh?"

Chapter 5

"With great power comes great responsibility". God, I hate that cliche, thought Guy Lambert after saying it out loud to nobody. People use it all the time now. Whether passing over the TV remote or the keys to an office building. Try running a seaside village. Try running it so the tourists love coming back. Try running it so that the residents don't want to leave or feel stressed by too many tourists. Try keeping the number of tourists low enough to be manageable but high enough to be profitable.

He looked out the window of the Town Hall Meeting Room as he waited for the committee to arrive and watched the early morning come to life. He looked to the right. Over the rooftop of his hotel he could see the beach and the sea. Not many about yet. Lunchtime people will eat on the benches or on the sand and dog walkers will enjoy the early April air. Joggers will be pleased that they have the use of such a beautiful beach. Still too early in the year for many weekday visitors. There's Johnson cleaning the beach anyway. Good man. We'll be ready for the beach inspection committee when they visit on Thursday with their Blue Flag again.

Straight ahead, across Town Hall Square, he saw old Bob cursing and swearing at the new sweeping contraption that Guy insisted he use. He bet the old bugger used his broom as soon as he was no longer in view. To the left all the pretty art deco houses cascaded up the hillside to Rose Park. There's the postie. What a round he has. He must love this area even though the hills are hard work. We're so far out he probably doesn't have another round. His relief postie must love it too. She's quite miserable most days though. Oh well each to their own.

The committee rotated every two months between April and November with volunteers making up a skeleton crew in the other months. This was the first time the new committee had met. From the beach end of the Town Square, Sergeant Scott Hayward, the local bobby, and Bill Fisher, the grocer, walked towards the Town

Hall. They seemed to be chatting amiably although Scott always seemed uncomfortable with Bill. Maybe the rumours of Bill's philandering with the farmers wives rested uneasily with Scott. Guy was certain that there was nothing to the rumours. A little mutual flirtation perhaps, but nothing more.

From the Rose Park side of the Town Square, came Maggie Marsh, owner of The Cream Team Cafe. A Rosegarden resident for nine years, she was the newest addition to the village. Known to all as the Immaculate Convention for her buttoned up, spick and span spinsterly appearance and personality, she was a staunch believer in the preservation of Rosegarden as a quaint old fashioned though liberal thinking village.

That's three of them, Guy thought as he scoured the streets looking for the other three. There's Ron Greening, retired gardener now acting as the voice of the residents. The villagers must be sick of Ron banging on their doors asking for their complaints. He must be sick of not receiving any. Ah, there's Charlie Osborne, huffing and puffing and waddling at double time. The owner, by default, of Caught In A Dream. Since his father retired at the end of the summer before last, Charlie took over the tourist gift shop. Guy wondered how it was going. He had noticed a fall in profits since the change. He really should visit the shops more. Oh good, here's Mama Cassandra with a food basket. Should be some lovely samples from her Caribbean restaurant. Descended from one of the first families to settle in his grandfather's idyllic village.

So we're all represented, he thought. Hotels and B&Bs, eateries, tourist shops, local shops and residents. Just one last look out the window at his heritage before everyone enters the room and the meeting starts.

*

The village council of Rosegarden decided, long ago, to only call meetings once every other month in the off season and then monthly when things got busy from Easter to August Bank

Holiday. Anything outside of that could be discussed over a coffee or a pint.

This was the pre-Easter get together and the first since that twenty minute chat in January at the Fisherman's Arms.

"Morning, all. Shall we get things started by talking about the schedule for..."

"Excuse me Mr Chairman but we haven't read last meeting's minutes or minuted who is present." Ron Greening was a stickler for the regulations.

Guy Lambert stared at him for a moment. "Ron, the last meeting lasted twenty minutes at the Fisherman's. There were no minutes as far as I'm aware. Unless you wrote them on a beer mat."

Ron shuffled in his seat. "Always most improper these meetings."

"Look, Ron, we write down what needs doing in our diaries. As far as who is here, we know Dr Jo is away visiting relatives this week. Everyone else is present. However, if you would like to minute take, then please note that this is the first meeting of this committee, apart from the winter volunteers and Sergeant Hayward who is expected to attend every meeting. You and Maggie were the only Winter volunteers."

"Thank you, Mr Chairman."

Guy disguised his dismay at the formality

"As I was about to say," he addressed the committee again, "we need to set up schedules for the upcoming season. Easter is next weekend and we expect many people will come to the village as always, including this Thursday when the clean beach people give us an inspection. Then, of course we'll have the May Bank Holiday, followed by the midsummer Folk Festival and Morris Dancing contest, Pride weekend, the jazz weekend, and the Rose Festival.

"We also need to discuss the shortlist for new resident applicants. We only have one family vacancy and one couple vacancy."

"It would be lovely to see some new faces." Beamed Mama Cassandra.

At that moment the door almost flew off its hinges as Captain Nightingale burst in.

He looked around the room and shouted out "The ice cream man is dead!"

"I know this one", laughed Charlie Osborne, "he was found covered with hundreds and thousands, raspberry sauce and a flake stuck in his ear. Police say he topped himself." Osborne laughed at his own joke very loudly. Nobody else did.

"This is serious. Frankie Flake has been murdered! His body is lying in his van as we speak. Danny and I photographed the scene. He managed some video on his phone too."

Everyone looked at each other and then at the Captain.

"What? My Danny?" asked Bill Fisher.

"Yes. After he delivered my groceries."

The Captain told them everything from the time he left his house.

"I hope you didn't damage our bike." said Fisher. "It's been in the family for generations"

"A man is dead and you're worried about a bike?" asked the Captain.

"Quite right, Captain" agreed Lambert. "Where's Danny now? Can we see the footage." Sergeant Hayward turned pale. He seemed to be trying to take it all in and figure out what to do.

"Looking after the shop for his mother. That's what he's supposed to be doing." Fisher said.

On cue, Danny came in with his iPhone held up like a sacred relic. An offering to all those in the room.

"Why aren't you at the shop?"

"Mum's ok. I phoned her and told her what happened. She's looking after the place, and Daisy too."

"Oh Christ. That's all we need! She better not eat everything."

"I fed her this morning." The Captain replied indignantly.

"How do you know he was talking about your dog?" Laughed Charlie Osborne. Again he was alone.

"You're lucky we're at this meeting, Osborne."

"Please, Bill. And you too, Charlie." demanded Lambert. "Come on, Danny, let's all see it."

"I have to warn you that some of it is gruesome."

"Yes Captain, we know" said Lambert looking round to make sure everyone agreed.

Maggie Marsh looked worried. "I'd rather not look if that's alright." She asked

"No. Nor me." Greening said.

"Fine, fine." Lambert said waving his hand dismissively. He was already engrossed in the slide show.

When they got to the corpse everyone gasped except the Captain and Danny. Then they watched the video.

"Shit!"

"My God!"

"Oh how awful" Maggie Marsh said with a shaky voice after curiosity got the better of her.

"What on earth should we do?" Greening had finally looked over everyone's shoulder.

"Why, phone the police of course!" Maggie sounded more confident now.

"Absolutely, we should." Agreed Greening.

"Now, now. Not so hasty" Lambert waved both palms at them to calm everyone. "Danny, you didn't tell your mum all the details did you? About the dead body I mean."

"No. The Captain said not too. I just said there had been some vandalism and I had photographed it."

"Good. Very good, Danny. Sergeant Hayward, you've been very quiet. What are your thoughts? Could you handle the investigation until after Easter?"

Looks were given between everyone suddenly understanding Lambert's concern. All looked at the Sergeant.

"Well, I don't know. Possibly. We should phone the County Police though. Nothing like this has happened in my thirty five years as the village policeman. I'm not quite sure what to do."

He sat down and gave it some thought while the others waited.

"I've never had to deal with more than a shoplifter in the gift shop. Someone bashing the change machine in the arcade.

"There will have to be a post mortem to determine the cause of death and forensics to work things out."

"I've seen you use a fingerprint kit, Scott. As for the autopsy surely that can be done after it's reported next week. In the mean time just ask questions around town. Doctor Jo could probably perform an autopsy when she gets back."

"I don't know, Guy. I've not had to ask many questions before. Like I said the worst that's happened is a shoplifter or accidental vandalism."

"There has been worse than that" Offered the Captain. "Those hoodlums on the beach, the vandals in the arcade and those louts shouting abuse in the Gutty Shark. That was sorted out."

"I didn't sort it out though." Scott said quietly looking down.

"No." Lambert grinned and looked around. "Tony Martini did." Everybody nodded.

Chapter 6

Captain Nightingale, Daisy, Sergeant Hayward and Danny climbed the stairs on the side of the building and entered the roof garden through an arch of silk bougainvillea. Tony Martini's roof garden was a pocket of Polynesia in the middle of an English seaside village. A jungle of potted palms, bamboo, fake tropical flowers, strings of bright lights that challenged the stars at night, fishermen's nets dotted with multi-coloured Japanese glass floats draped over the walls, plastic flamingos that vied for space with terracotta replicas of Easter Island men and wooden Tikis.

Tony sat at a table in the middle of this paradise dressed in chinos, closed toe sandals and an Hawaiian shirt printed with red and white block patterns. In front of him were the remnants of breakfast. He held an unlit cigar between the fingers of one hand and an iPhone that he was staring at with manic eyes in the other.

"C'mon. C'mon. C'mon." He was chanting at it.

"Morning, Tony!" The Captain said cheerfully.

Tony held up the cigar hand in a stop gesture and growled "C'mon" at his phone a little louder as if in competition with the Captain. His eyes never left the screen.

"Sorry to disturb, Tony" offered Sergeant Hayward.

Once more the stop hand came up and the shouts of "C'mon" got louder and more regular.

The visitors looked at each other and thought this wasn't such a great idea. Then Tony gave a shout of "Yes! Get in you beauty!" and turned around to his audience. "I won!" He shouted with a grin.

"Well done, Tony! Knew you would. Bit early for the races though?"

Tony gave a blank look and then laughed. "No, Captain. It's ebay. I won a Shaheen shirt on ebay. Absolute bloody bargain too."

He got blank faces all round. Nobody shrugged their shoulders but they may as well.

"A designer of Hawaiian shirts. Well, the fabric that's used to make them."

Still not a flicker of recognition.

"Next time you see the Elvis album, Blue Hawaii, look at his shirt. It's a Shaheen.

Anyway gentlemen, how can I help?"

"Well it's something of an ugly and sticky situation, Tony" said the Captain.

"Literally sticky" added Danny.

"OK, hold on. Everyone grab a pew. I'll get this lot cleared away and get us all some coffee" Tony reached under the table and spoke into a ceramic hibiscus on his left hand side and then reached down to scratch behind Daisy's ear, she rolled over and showed him her belly.

"Yes, Uncle?" Came a crackly female voice from somewhere unknown. Danny looked around for speakers and saw none.

"Can you bring up four coffees and take away the breakfast stuff please, Peggy? Oh and if there are any little pieces of sausage in the kitchen, meat sausage not my veggie ones, bring some up."

"OK"

"I hope that's OK with you Captain?"

"Oh Absolutely, Yes of course. This really is a marvellous set up you have here, Tony. I can't even tell where you've hidden the speaker we just heard Peggy through." The Captain smiled and winked.

"Oh I almost forgot!" said Tony and he reached below the table again and this time cicadas and tropical birds could be heard. It was done well without being too loud or constant. Daisy sat up and cocked her head.

Peggy came up with the coffee, cream, sugar and little pieces of sausage. She looked at Danny and smiled. "Hi, Danny"

"Hello, Peggy." He smiled and kept her gaze.

Tony looked from one to the other. "Alright, alright. Blimey. Get a room. After you finish work though. Speaking of which, how come you're not at the shop or delivering? Your dad will blow a gasket if he finds out."

Peggy cleared the breakfast things and left.

"Young Danny here has helped me this morning and his dad knows where he is. He's not happy but, well, these are unique circumstances."

"I think everyone's way ahead of me here." He said placing the saucer of sausage down for Daisy.

"Yes. Well this morning Danny used his phone to take photos and video of a crime scene I discovered. A serious crime. It involves one of your employees. Frankie Flake."

"Frankie? Oh Christ. I knew it was a mistake letting him work here again. What did he do?"

"He got murdered." Danny said.

*

Tony flicked through the photos on Danny's phone, frowning in concentration. He got out his iPad. "Airdrop these to my iPad will you, Danny"

"Yeah sure"

The Captain looked on, amazed at the technology. Tony looked at the larger photos on his iPad.

"It's hard to think who would want to kill Frankie" Sergeant Hayward said. "I can't imagine he had any enemies."

"Well he had at least one or he wouldn't look like that" Tony said pointing to a photo of the dead man face down in ice cream. "The real police force, no offence, Scott, the real police force should be involved in this."

"None taken. I agree but we're outvoted on this. I'm going to have a lot of explaining to do after Easter." He said shaking his head. "Let's see if we can sort this out as much as possible. Maybe even solve it. Then we can go to the County Police more confidently."

"Shit. Alright. Look, first thing we can ask ourselves around this table, when did we last see Frankie? I saw him yesterday at midday when he started his shift. How about you, Danny?"

"Erm, must have been one or just after. I had a lunch picnic by the beach and saw him serving a couple of people. I can't remember who. I was with Peggy. She might remember."

Tony smiled. There were worse people his niece could be with than Danny. "I'll ask her. How about you Sergeant?"

"I was driving back from my farm rounds that I usually do on a Sunday afternoon. Best time to get them all at home and catch up. Anyway it was about twenty past six and I drove past his ice cream van and looked across. Frankie wasn't in it."

"So he may have already have been dead on the floor." said Tony. "Could you tell if the engine was running?"

"No. I'm afraid not."

"OK. Captain?"

The Captain looked puzzled by the question, as if he was trying hard to figure it out. "It was the beginning of my evening walk, it must have been about half five I guess." He looked from Tony to Scott and back again. "I waved hello to him and he waved back. He looked bored or fed up."

"OK, so some time between five thirty and six thirty he was killed or at least absent from his van. Second thing. Did any of us really know him? Or even know anything about him?" Tony looked around at a few thoughtful faces. "OK, I'll start." He looked at one of the pictures of Frankie's corpse as if he was looking for more information. "Old Alfredo, not long before he died, asked me to get in touch with his only relative, Francis, or Frankie Flake as we know him. They were the only relatives each other had and Frankie wasn't easy to track down. Alfredo was worried about Frankie keeping bad company, for good reason, and said I should consider him to take over the old boy's ice cream van. The seaside, especially in our village, would do him good. Guy agreed to it but only for seasonal work. Well, Frankie and I had a few words last summer. Nothing drastic but enough to piss him off. He was always on his phone and often kept customers waiting while he scrolled. I put a stop to it by banning it from his van. At the end of last summer he vowed never to return but came back a couple of weeks ago. I can't say I knew much about him personally. He was difficult to warm to and I didn't try too hard. What do you know about him Danny?"

"Well me and Peggy used to get ice cream from him. We felt sorry for him because Connie got all the business with the Mr Whippy style ice cream. Nobody wanted the scoop stuff. He always smiled at Peggy and chatted a little to us. Not about anything in particular. Just small talk. Mainly compliments for Peggy. But small talk too."

"Yes, sounds like my experiences. Chap never had much to say. Wanted to know if a man my age still cared for the ladies. Dashed cheek of it. Other than that just small talk."

"I used to ask him how things were. Just from a professional, police point of view. He used to say fine and nothing to report. That was it. I didn't feel comfortable with him. Pretty sure he didn't feel comfortable with me either. Not sure why."

"Right. So, basically, he was a mystery man. Nobody knows or knew anything about him. That's something we'll have to look into, Scott. Ask around the village and the people who he shared digs with.

"Well, Danny, thanks for the photos and video but you better go back to work. Captain, go about your normal business. You always talk and listen to people. Keep your ears open and see if you hear anything unusual, or about Frankie, at all. The official line, and I'm sure Guy will agree with this, is that Frankie's gone missing. His death should be kept secret for now. He smashed up his van and did a runner.

"Scott, you and I will go back to the scene of the crime. Let's hope nobody's pissed around with anything."

Chapter 7

Tony picked up some food bags and vinyl gloves from the restaurant kitchen and met up with Scott on the promenade, and the two fast walked to the crime scene.

It was getting warm with a gentle sea breeze that spread the briny fragrance far inland. Here and there, small clouds braved the Spring sunshine which had evaporated others like them. Most of the residents of the village had started their working week. A few of those who weren't working walked and waded along the beach. Dogs, tethered to their humans, greeted each other with rear end sniffs and let their owners chat about the weekend that had just finished.

Tony looked around him and took in the scene along the shore.

"Although my family have lived here for generations, I never fail to feel lucky to live in a place like this."

"Yes. It's lovely." Sergeant Hayward answered vaguely.

Tony waited until they were past the Seaview Hotel and asked "What went on in that meeting, Scott? How come you didn't put your foot down and call the proper authorities? We're probably going to be in over our heads. God knows what we'll find".

"What happened? Guy Lambert is what happened. I knew I couldn't handle this so I said we should phone the county police. Lambert was certain that wouldn't be good for the village. Especially with Easter at the end of the week and the Blue Flag people before that. I crumbled. Nobody has confidence in me. Not even me. They said we should put you in charge because you're more effective than me. I didn't argue."

Tony couldn't decide on being proud or saying words to pick up his friend. In the end he said, "C'mon, Scott. Don't beat yourself up. Everyone in the village likes and respects you."

"No. They respect the uniform."

They were getting to the edge of the buildings and closer to the car park. Scott grabbed Tony's arm and they stopped. "I have no idea what I'm doing, Tony. I've never been in this situation. I had high hopes and big dreams when I got out of training. I was going all the way to the top. Chief Constable via Detective solving crimes and putting the bad ones behind bars. Turns out I wasn't good enough and I didn't know how to improve or shine as a PC. They posted me here over thirty years ago to replace the Sergeant who retired. I got his rank and his house. Sergeant to nobody. I'm out of the way here. I'm on an outpost where nothing happens. The worse that happens is an occasional punch up at The Fisherman's or hooligans on the beach, and those are once in a blue moon. When that happens they call you. I've never seen a crime scene, let alone investigated one."

Tony got beside him and put his arm around Scott's shoulder. "I've never seen a crime scene. Only on telly. It's going to be fine. The stupid bastard probably slipped on ice cream and knocked himself unconscious and died or something. Anyway, whatever happens, we'll learn together. Now let's get over there. Frankie's probably floating in ice cream by now."

They stopped at the entrance to the car park and compared the scene to the photo on the iPad. It looked the same.

They put on the vinyl gloves and went to each of the items that had been photographed.

The pile of cigarette butts seemed to be in a neat pile. Tony looked through them and put the butts in a plastic baggy and sealed it. There was just one brand of cigarettes.

"It's either two people who often drive around together or a one-off meeting where they both chain smoked. Or one person who rarely empties the ashtray." Tony said looking over at the beer bottles. The next point of interest.

"Looks like they tipped out the ashtray. Like they were cleaning the car." suggested Scott.

"Yeah. Could be. Must be an old car. How many cars have ashtrays now?"

"Maybe, they kept an ashtray handy for long trips. There's ten butts here. Where do you start with stuff like this?"

They walked to the beer bottles. There were nine, all the same brand, stood up next to the low wall that marked the edge of the car park. The bottles were spaced evenly apart and all the labels faced exactly the same way.

"OCD drunks. That's weird. If they had equal amounts of beer then that was three each. Two people in the car, three people drinking beer on the wall." Tony was thinking about this and looking around the area.

"Or one person who drank all nine bottles." said Scott.

"Or nine people who had one each. Or any bloody combination. Shit. When we finish this first look around get your fingerprint kit and I'll get some people to guard the area. If we can't identify who the people are, at least we can identify how many there were."

Tony phoned the direct number to the restaurant kitchen "Who's that, Benny? Right you and all the waiters be at the East car park, pronto. Capiche?

"What do you mean who is this? Me. Tony Martini. Your bloody boss unless you stop farting around. Then I'll be the bloke who fired you.

"Twat." He looked at Scott and shook his head. "Speaking of which I better phone Lambert. Let him know we're closing the car park.

"Hey, Guy, it's me, Tony Martini. That's right, stirred but never shaken." He looked at Scott and gave the wanker sign and shook his head. "Just to let you know, we're closing the East car park for a couple of hours. Alright? Cool. I'll let you know how we're getting on when I have more to go on. Yeah, you too. Bye.

"Lambert can be such a twat at times. Right let's have a look at Frankie and the van."

The first thing they noticed when they got inside the cab was the knife. It was missing.

Chapter 8

"Come on, let's get you home, old girl."

They walked back along the beach to avoid any cars that may be on the one and only road in to Rosegarden. The Captain wondered what he could do to help the situation. A murder in the village. Nothing bad ever happened in Rosegarden, let alone murder. A few squabbles now and then that were usually settled over a cup of tea with adjudicators. There were rumours of extra marital affairs now and then. Nothing was ever confirmed or admitted and people often forgot about things after a while. Except Bill Fisher and Molly, wife of Laurie Beale the farmer.

Molly was a lovely person. Beautiful and sexy, intellectual and smart, funny and flirtatious, even with the Captain. He doubted she ever followed it up with anyone and she knew how to make a man back off, with either a joke or a warning. Molly always went back to Laurie with a guilt free conscience.

Bill Fisher visited there often but maybe just because being in her company was a pleasure.

Could some sort of misunderstanding like that lead to a death? Perhaps.

Daisy met up with another dog and the Captain looked up out of his thoughts and saw Jack Dhaji and Sandy

"Good morning Jack!"

"Morning Captain. Look at those two."

Daisy and Sandy took it in turns to chase each other.

"They'll be tired out and sleep for the rest of the day at that rate. Daisy will anyway."

"Sandy will too."

They watched the dogs play for a minute.

"You didn't walk Sandy near the east car park, last night did you?"

"Yes I did, why?"

"Did you see anything strange?"

"Saw and heard." Jack seemed excited to tell someone about it. "First, when I was watching telly I heard an exhausted ice cream van die."

"Really?"

"Yes then, later on, when I was walking Sandy, a dark car turned left in to the car park and then, on our way back, the same car turned right in to the car park from the village."

"Very strange. Did you recognise it as a car from around here?"

"No. That said, not many have a car around here; I'm surprised Emma still has a business. I guess it ticks over."

"Yes. At least nobody in Rosegarden needs to make a big profit."

"What made you ask, Cap?"

"Well, I heard the same as well. I've found out Frankie Flake has gone missing."

"No kidding. I saw him yesterday. He was having a right go at Ron Greening. I never thought they were buddies, but that was quite the argument."

"What were they arguing about?"

"I don't know. I couldn't hear the words, just the tone and I saw them pointing at each other. You know? Angry finger pointing, and all."

"Ron and Frankie? What on earth? I think Frankie has gone off to parts unknown."

"Not too far I hope. He owes me twenty quid. A few others are waiting to be paid back as well."

"How many others?"

"That I know of? About ten. Who knows how many more."

"Could be the reason he left. Could be the reason Ron argued with him."

The two men said their farewells and the dogs had a final sniff then the Captain and Daisy walked along the beach. They passed the crime scene and the Captain noticed nothing had changed. Looking back he saw Tony and Scott in the distance walking towards the van.

He'd make his way back and then report to them. Motives and suspects were in plentiful supply.

Chapter 9

"Shit! A great bit of evidence like that and it's gone missing."

"Not to worry, Scott."

"What do you mean? The knife's missing. It might be the murder weapon."

"I doubt it," Tony said smiling, "that's Glen May's knife. He may be a vandal and a joyrider and a wannabe hard case and many other things, but I doubt he would kill anyone. If push came to shove he'd shit himself and run in a fight."

"How do you know it's his knife?"

Tony opened up his iPad and pointed at the knife that Danny photographed. "Because it's one of a kind and I sold it to him. I told him if he used it in a crime in our village I'd use it to cut off his haemorrhoids followed by his balls. I'll pay him a visit later. Right let's see what else is here."

Scott couldn't help but think that Tony was the right man for the job. He'd take a backseat and do whatever he said.

"Ever seen anyone use that glasses case, Scott?"

"No, I don't recognise it."

"Me either."

He picked it up. It was metal with a hinged lid. He weighed it in his palm.

"Christ! That would protect a pair of specs getting crushed by a tank driven by an elephant." He opened it, raised his eyebrows and pulled out the contents.

"You'd see all sorts after smoking some of these, including elephants driving tanks" Tony laughed and held up four joints.

"Frankie's?"

"More likely to be Glen May's or Glen May's mate's. That's if he wasn't here alone. I don't know. I'll bag it up and you can fingerprint it later.

"Let's see how much diesel is in the tank" He turned the ignition and got nothing. "No diesel, no battery. The engine must have been running a while. Then again it's an old van with an old battery. What's in the glove compartment?"

Scott opened the glove compartment "A camera and a notebook with his takings and some other scribblings. Like a code or something."

"Really? Let's have a look. Hm. No idea what all that is. I'll have a look later." He put it in his back pocket. "What else we got?"

Two packs of chewing gum, a can of Coke and a packet of crisps."

Tony looked at Scott and got hold of the access door to the serving area. "Alright, here we go."

The smell was much stronger now. The last of the ice cream had melted and leaked out, giving the appearance that Frankie had drowned in it. It was up to his close cropped sideburns. The serving area was getting warm. A couple of flies did an Argentinian Tango in mid air and swooped down every now and then. Whether they were going crazy for the corpse or the sticky pool on the floor, who knew.

"I should have bought him an up to date ice cream van. This one first served the Virgin Mary during her pregnancy cravings. It's not even a proper ice cream van - it's a converted luton. If it wasn't for all that ice cream everywhere our jobs would be a lot easier now."

"I have to say, Tony, you don't seem that bothered by Frankie's death." Scott was still in the cab, waiting for Tony to move up and buying time so he could prepare himself for the sight of Frankie's lifeless body.

"Well I didn't know him that well. He started in the middle of the summer, last year as you know. I was surprised when he came back this year. Like I said back at my place, I tore him a new arsehole for having a phone in the van and I also had a few complaints from some women about him making inappropriate comments, I ripped him a new one for that as well. When he came back this year I was a little reluctant to have him back but he said he would behave himself. I was going to just have the one van this year but thought, what the hell, may as well give him the benefit of the doubt and try to make a little extra for the village."

Tony straightened up and paused and thought. "The people of this village, and some of the visitors for that matter, are close knit and look out for each other. He lived with my staff and worked with my family. He never talked to anyone or joined in with anything. He must have upset somebody really bad to end up face down in ice cream. I look after my sisters girls, Connie and Peggy, and my cousin Paul. I have a duty to them to make sure they don't have a bad life and to prepare them to one day take over my business, if they want it. When someone like Frankie comes along and upsets people I have to ask who has he upset so much that he's wearing ice cream for cologne? A member of my staff? My nieces or cousin? Or just someone of the village I think highly of.

"So, to answer your question, I'm sad someone died but not enough to lose any sleep. Perhaps, in this case, it's a question of feeling for the person who killed him"

Scott gave that a few moments thought. "I think I understand what you mean. But you do know whoever did this should be brought to justice. Has to be, really, I mean the police would expect it. If we didn't do that, how would we even start to separate ourselves from the killer? And if we acted like that how would we cover something like this up?"

Tony looked at him seriously. "We have to take things as they happen.

"Here, come back here and help me turn him over." Tony worked his way to the back of the van and squatted by the dead man's feet.

Scott stood at the doorway staring down at the scene. He looked ill.

"What's the matter? C'mon. He's not going to turn himself over."

"I've never seen a corpse before."

"No?"

"You have, haven't you, Tony?"

"Ask me no questions, I'll tell you no lies."

"Oh God, no." He turned away to compose himself. "OK I can do this."

Scott squatted and put his hands under Frankie's shoulders.

"Alright, after three turn him over, to the right. One, two, three."

They both turned him over to their right like they were trying to twist him in the middle.

"Woah! Sorry Scott. My right, towards the window. One, two, three."

They flipped him over like a sausage on a barbecue. What they could see of his body was totally rigid from rigour mortis and discoloured, the rest was caked in ice cream.

Scott turned even paler. "Oh God. I'm going to throw up."

"Well do it on the beach, not on the. Oh. Too late. Oh well at least it's on the passenger side of the cab. When you can, come back and have a look. I may miss something."

He looked at the floor around the body first. It looked like a lot of blood mixed with the ice cream. A wasp did a crazy dance to the buzzing it made in the sticky mess and then lazily rose to the level of the window where it bashed its head trying to get out. Tony rose up and opened the serving hatch to let the smell, warm stale air and the wasp out. It drunkenly slammed against the surfaces for a few minutes then found its way outside.

Nothing looked out of place around Frankie. Tony studied the corpse from the head down. They would have to wash him for sure. There was no coroner but they could look for obvious bruising and to try and see what the weapon may have looked like. Maybe Doctor Jo could have a look when she got back.

There was a bruise on Frankie's face that looked fresh. Possibly from the fall. He looked around for a cloth or something to wipe the ice cream away. There was no sign of Scott. He noticed a cloth and roll of blue tissue on a shelf and used it to wipe Frankie's face. There seemed to be a little blood in the nose. Again probably from the fall. He raised himself and looked at the counter. There was blood there, mainly in one place with only a little splatter. He returned to the corpse and wiped the front of the white jacket. A thick layer of ice cream came off and, underneath, the jacket was red with blood. Tony ripped open the shirt and wiped the chest. There was a perfectly circular hole in line with the, now defunct, heart. A small wound with a lot of blood. Frankie must have lay unconscious while bleeding to death. It definitely wasn't a knife wound and it was too small for a bullet hole. What the hell was it?

Tony grabbed a few big gulps of fresh air outside the ice cream van. It wasn't so much the corpse and melted ice cream as Scott's vomit that made him want the sea breeze up his nostrils and in his lungs. He'd had to manoeuvre past it to get out the van.

He looked toward the village and saw the troop from his restaurant marching towards him. He waved at them and lit the cigar he'd been carrying around all morning. They waved back and most smiled. Mike and Paul never laughed or smiled. If he needed back up in a tough situation, he chose them. Most people backed off or quietened down when they saw two giant men, emotionless, expressionless and generally menacing, glaring at them. Truth be told, even though most people saw Tony as a Mafia type, often in an Hawaiian shirt and smoking a cigar, with henchmen who looked like killers, he ran a family restaurant and those two were a waiter and a chef. It's a pity that some people still believe in stereotypes and judge by using preconceived first impressions. Whether that's race, gender, age, sexuality or ethnicity. Tony had always used it to his benefit, though. People thought he was a crook or a gangster or a womaniser who ate pasta and drank red wine while listening to opera or Dean Martin. Let them believe in cliches as long as it got things done.

People prejudged Scott by his profession. The tourists saw him as some sort of cross between Poirot, traffic warden and old school Bobby on the beat. He got annoyed at all those assumptions and more annoyed by the way the people of Rosegarden saw him. Tony really hoped that this case, if you could call it that, would help Scott.

Where the bloody hell was Scott? He thought he heard a movement on the beach. He looked around the edge of the van and saw Scott on all fours facing away from him and toward the sand dunes.

"Not all the views from here are nice. Not still puking are you, Scott?"

"Tony look at this." He said pointing at something metallic on the the ground in front of him

"What you got?" He squatted next to Scott, being careful not to step in the second pile of vomit. "Bugger me!"

"Exactly."

"Where the hell did that come from?"

"Frankie?"

"No I checked him over."

They looked at the side of the van. There was a small hole in it, just above the coral painted on the side. It was meant to be a subaquatic paradise scene with an octopus and a sunken pirate's treasure chest. Here and there bright fish smiled out at people on the beach.

"What the hell." Tony looked at Scott. Scott looked back.

"Let's look at the other side."

They walked around the other side. Tony's staff kept their distance and waited by the entrance of the car park for Tony's signal to come down.

Tony and Scott studied the van. There, between a clownfish's eyes, was a hole almost identical to the other.

"Looks like we might be after a gunman after all."

Chapter 10

Everyone had their jobs. Mike, Benny and Peggy guarded the road entrance to the car park and Paul, Larry and Louisa guarded the beach entrances. Anthony went to the hardware store to buy string and the thinnest bamboo rod they had.

Scott went back to the station which, was in fact, his house, to get all his Crime Scene paraphernalia and Tony went to May's Garage.

May's had been in the village since the beginning. The first Guy Lambert's 1920 Sunbeam, the delivery vans throughout the decades, farm vehicles, either at the garage or at the farms were all repaired and serviced by the Mays. Every MOT of every vehicle since the 1920's had been done at May's as well as emergency work for the visiting tourists. It had been handed down through the generations. The Mays always said they had petrol and oil in their veins.

When Tony got there he saw a mechanic bent over an engine, greasy towel hanging out the back pocket of their overalls. Now and then a remembered phrase would be sung along with the radio and then turn to a mumble as soon as the lyrics failed them.

"I'd recognise that shape and beautiful singing voice anywhere, overalls or not"

Emma May stepped back and stood up. "Tony!" She said turning round. "This is a pleasant surprise on a Monday morning. What you doing here?"

"Apart from looking at a woman who makes boiler suits look sexy?"

"Enough of that nonsense. You don't have a car so you don't need an MOT or service. I'm not complaining though, I rarely see you. You work at night and I work in the day."

There was a pause and a moment and a smile in each other's eyes that they both saw.

"And we're both busy business owners. Tell you what though, if I can borrow a litre of diesel and Glen with some jump leads and a van, you can have five free meals at my restaurant."

"I don't like eating out on my own."

"I'll eat with you. I'll throw in all the wine you can drink."

"You don't have that many bottles."

They both chuckled.

"OK. You didn't have to throw in five meals but I'll accept the offer of one. What's up? One of your ice cream vans broken down?"

"Yeah. Frankie's. I think he left it running and left town or something. You didn't hear anything strange last night did you?"

"No. I was too engrossed in Sweet Home Alabama and an Indian take away from Sanjiv Gupta's."

"Nice! Sounds like a nice night in. Hang on, is he open on Sundays?"

"No, but I had a look at his delivery tuk-tuk, and the homemade takeaway was on the house."

"Nice trade. Anyway, do you know much about Frankie?"

"Not really. He's quiet and I never really go for his ice cream. I prefer Mr Whippy"

"Fair enough."

Emma went to the entrance to the garage and called out for Glen.

"He won't be a minute."

*

Glen gave Tony sidelong glances as he loaded up the jump leads and diesel in his van. Tony remained silent until they drove out the garage and waved at Emma.

"Alright, Glen, what happened last night?"

"I don't know what you mean, To-, Mr Martini."

"Don't piss me around. Your knife, the one I sold you, was photographed at a crime scene but when me and Sergeant Hayward got there it was missing."

"Shit"

"Exactly. So?"

Glen drove slowly to the car park thinking about his options.

"I'm waiting, Glen. We'll be there soon. I want to know."

"Alright. Me and Glen West were drinking beers on the beach,"

"Oh God, the great double act, The Two Glens."

"and Glen goes up toward the car park for a piss. He said Frankie Flake's Ice Cream van was left in the car park. We were both drunk on beers and high on joints. We thought maybe we could nick some ice cream. We had the munchies. I know what you said about the knife, Mr Martini, but it wasn't a violent crime. I was going to force the lock on the van doors but they were open. So we got inside the cab and tried to force the door to the serving area but it wouldn't budge."

"It pulls. It doesn't push open"

"Fuck's sake"

They reached the car park and Mike and Peggy stepped aside.

"What's going on?"

"You'll see in a minute, Glen. Park just here while you tell me the rest of your story. You were trying to curb your munchies with ice cream and being a twat with the door"

Glen looked hurt.

"I'm waiting again, Glen."

"Yeah I couldn't figure the door but Glen shouts out that the keys are in the ignition. So, being a little stoned we decided to go for a joyride in the ice cream van. We got as far as the entrance and then the diesel and battery seemed to die. Just as well really. We couldn't figure how to turn off the bloody music."

Tony laughed. "Sorry. Go on."

"Well the van rolled back and only stopped because of the lamp post. We got out and ran. That's it."

"What a pair of twats. I want the knife back. I'll refund you."

Glen pouted and sulked.

"Did you go home straight away?"

"Yeah. We went our different ways and went straight home."

"What time did you get home?"

"Mum was in the bathroom doing her thing before bed, so between half ten and eleven".

"Right. When we get out I want you to look around and tell me if there's anything different."

They got out. They were parked just inside the entrance and Glen pointed to the beer bottles.

"Those look like the ones we drank but ours were on the beach."

Tony gave him a hard smack on the back of the head that made Glen's eyes water.

"What the fuck, Tony"

Tony gave him another two. "The first was for littering the beach. The second was for swearing at me. The third was for calling me Tony."

Glen's eyes were watery and he looked like a ten year old whose just been grounded for a week.

"Were there any cigarette butts in a pile in the middle of the car park. Around the third bay in the middle."

Glen gave it some thought. "No, Mr Martini."

"Alright, Glen." He turned and looked at the ice cream van. "Glen? Where was the van parked when you first got in it?"

Glen pointed to its usual position. "Just over there. The way it always is." Perpendicular to how it ended up and facing the sand dunes so its sides faced the sea and the road with the serving hatch on the car park side.

"And Frankie Flake? Was he anywhere in sight?"

"No Mr Martini. If he was we wouldn't have tried anything."

Chapter 11

"What a morning, eh, Daisy?" Captain Nightingale sat in his relaxation chair and looked out to sea while sipping a cup of tea. Daisy lay on the window seat in the bay window and started to nod off.

"That's a great life you live, Daisy. Sleep when you want, everything provided for you and not a care in the world. In the next life let me come back as a well looked after dog. I wonder where Frankie is bound on his next life. Does it correspond to where you were in previous lives or is it just a merry-go-round that never stops and you get on where you can and hope the ride lasts for as long as possible so you don't have to start all over again. Who threw Frankie off the ride? It's unimaginable that anyone from this village did. Did he owe that much money? You don't kill over small amounts. Most normal people don't kill over large amounts, but there he was face down in ice cream. Tony and Scott will probably do a good job. But will they solve it?"

The Captain drained the last of his tea and looked at the cup longingly. That was a great cuppa.

"Alright old girl, you look after the place and I'll put on my deerstalker and get out the meerschaum and pretend I'm Sherlock. Don't worry, I'll be home for your dinner time."

Daisy raised her head at the word dinner then went back to sleep again.

The day had become a little warmer and the Captain took his sweater off his shoulders and walked in to Rosegarden. Along the shore the sea stretched out into a light blue that almost matched the sky except for the underlying greyness. The sky was now cloudless and ever decreasing shadows told all who saw them it was almost lunchtime. As he neared Rosegarden, the sight of the pretty village had the same effect on him that it always did, a smile came to his face and a feeling of peace washed over him. This gave way only a little as he caught sight of the cordoned off car park with Tony's restaurant staff stood guarding all the entrances. Good old Tony. As the cliche went, solid as a rock. A little rough like a rock maybe, but the sea and sand and breeze of Rosegarden had smoothed even his hardened edges. The Captain had never delved in to Tony's past but he knew there were some years spent away from Rosegarden. 'Missing years' some people called that period. Nobody spoke much about it but it was over when the Captain arrived in Rosegarden. Tony was the man he now knew. Previous lives were a person's right to keep to themselves or exploit them as they chose. Reinvention is often a good thing.

The Captain looked over at the ice cream van and noticed Tony and Scott and others with a bamboo rod in the van. Hmm, a trajectory calculation, I suppose, he thought. He was going to go over and tell them what Jack Dhaji had said but decided that could wait. Best not disturb them. Besides, he had his own detective work to do.

Rosegarden got bigger now. The overall view of it gave way to close ups of the beautiful art deco buildings. The outlying houses that led to the main promenade were painted in the same white and subdued mint green as the rest of the village. They were one bedroom bungalows with small front and back gardens and the cheapest of all the houses. They also had the easiest access and best view of the beach. The houses at the top of the hill which, belonged to the Lamberts, had a panoramic view and were large but were an uphill climb from the beach and with the garages situated in the middle level of the village, driving to the top was not an option.

He crossed over the road that led up the hill towards the tourist shops and looked over to the beach. The sight of the Fab Four, who were seated on one of the promenade benches, made him smile. He went over to talk to them.

The name was given to them in the sixties because Joan, Paula, Georgia and Reno sounded too much like the original Fab Four, for it not to be used.

Joan and Paula were the first couple to have a same sex marriage in the county. That is the first official same sex marriage. The original Guy Lambert unofficially married them in the House of Worship in 1953 in a ceremony he wrote for the occasion. Georgia and Reno, second generation Rosegardeners, were married a year later by the same person in the same place but with a slightly different service. Georgia's parents were white South Africans and Reno's parents were black Jamaicans. Neither sets of parents were opposed to the wedding but, back then, people in nearby villages and towns still had prejudices and suspicions of everything and everyone to do with Rosegarden.

"Hey, look. It's young Captain Nightingale."

The Captain was bombarded with a chorus of enthusiastic Good Mornings and smiles.

"Ha. The only people in the village who regard me as young."

"Compared to us, you are, dear." Paula smiled. The Captain noticed that she and Joan still held hands. Even after all those years together. Both were mid century glamorous in a beatnik sort of way. Both wore turtleneck black sweaters, Paula with black jeans and Joan with wide slacks in a Prince of Wales check. Paula wore a bob and Joan Close cropped hair beneath a beret. For any age they were healthy and for theirs they were amazing. The same could be said for Georgia and Reno. They, too, were glamorous in a yesteryear kind of way. Reno chose chinos with a white t-shirt and windbreaker topped with a Panama, and Georgia wore beach pyjamas with a shawl over the top and a wide brimmed sun hat. All four wore sunglasses.

"How ya doing, Captain? Tried that rum yet. It's a sipper not a mixer."

"I did, thank you, Reno. It was divine and I can't wait to have my next one. I'm not an alcoholic though, so I will wait."

They all chuckled then looked out to sea.

"I don't suppose any of you heard or saw anything strange last night?"

"A deflating electronic opera singer belting out 'Donna e mobile'. We would have gone out to look but Miles Davis had our full attention." Paula said and looked over her shades.

"You two are such beatniks still. We heard it while having a wine at the Crow's Nest. A few went outside and spotted the two Glens running from the car park. When we left we saw Pearl and Dean walking from the dunes and looking over. They went their own ways after that. Not the most likely couple in the village, but then who is?"

The four and the Captain all nodded.

"Why do you ask, Captain?"

"Frankie Flake is missing and his van was found in a weird position."

"Frankie is weird if you ask me." Said Joanna.

"Pervy, darling not weird."

"Both I'd say."

"Why is that?" Asked the Captain.

"Well he is harmless, I suppose. Just sees himself as a Latin lover but without the charm or know-how to pull it off. He's weird in a not wonderful way. I don't know. Just creepy weird."

"Wanted to know the size of my schlong. Asked me once. Asked if all black men were well hung. Told him to categorise was wrong and to mind his own bloody business."

Georgia chuckled and the rest followed.

"I would sometimes see him in heated arguments when he was here. Either with women or their partners or people he owed money to. But sometimes he would be so quiet and dejected looking "

"Did he argue with anyone in particular?"

"No, Captain. Not that I can think of."

"What about Tony Martini?" asked Paula. "He ripped him a new one on many occasion."

"Yes but he never gave it back though." Joan said.

"True."

"Charlie Osborne was his friend but I saw them go at it recently."
"Is that so, Reno? Do you know what was said?"
"Something about Charlie telling someone about Frankie and an iPad or iPhone or something. I don't know exactly what"
"You know, I think Frankie was full of bluff and bluster, but if someone had mistakenly thought of him as serious that could be a dangerous situation." added Paula.
"Which is why I thought the argument with Charlie stood out. They're the only ones who laughed at each others jokes."
"That's very interesting. Thank you for the chat, everyone. It's been very informative."
The Captain had plenty to report back.

Chapter 12

Scott returned to the car park with his evidence kit. It had been a very long time since it had seen the light of day and he had to check twice to remember what should be in there. He had handled the fingerprint brushes and boxes of powder and tape like an archaeologist examining old bones or teeth or coins. He tried hard to remember everything he had been taught all those years ago, long before outside agencies did forensics. He waved to Tony as Mike and Peggy let him through the entrance.

"What did you find out, Tony?"

Tony gave him a brief run down of what Glen told him.

"What do you think?"

"Either Frankie went off to get something when the Glens were messing around and then some OCD person shot him or he was already dead. But then the bullet we found would have been somewhere else. It's confusing."

"We need a timeline. Without a coroner that's a little difficult." He gave it some thought then got out his phone.

"Hey, Siri." His phone came to life. "How long does it take for a body to become fully stiffened with rigour mortis?"

After a pause, a jerky electronic voice answered "Here's what I found about, how long is a body compared to a surfboard?"

"What? Seriously? I hate it when it does that." He typed the question in while Scott tried to stop laughing. "Alright, it wasn't that bloody funny.

"Looks like he's been dead at least twelve hours. Let's put my TV detective viewing to some use."

"You going all Poirot on me now?"

"No, Scott. Joe Kenda."

Not for the first time that day he was met with a blank expression.

"Joe Kenda. Homicide Hunter. 'If you kill, I will find you'"

And still no recognition showed on Scott's face.

"Oh well. He's a real life detective with a very high solve rate. From Colorado Springs in America. He studies the crime scene and gets a lot of information. One thing we can do is see the path of the bullet."

Anthony had just come back from the hardware store.

"Anthony. Bring that stuff to the van, please."

Tony took the bamboo rod from Anthony. It was two metres long and ten millimetres in diameter. He put it in the side of the van through the bullet hole then passed it over to Scott and, for the second time dodged vomit, to get in the back of the van. Stepping around Frankie and squelching in melted ice cream, he got in line with the rod and looked to see where it had entered. He opened up the ice cream compartment to see the bamboo poking in.

"It went through the ice cream freezer." He told Scott and then pulled it through and found the next hole, about forty centimetres above the floor, that had gone unnoticed. The rod found the exit hole between two shelves on the other side. Tony slid it in and stood up at the serving hatch. "If it did hit Frankie it would have hit his thigh. If he was squatting down to hide and got hit, it would have gone through him. Neither of those things happened.

Tony thought for a minute.

"Let's wrap the string around the end and pull it straight to see where they fired from. I think I know though."

They carried out the experiment and the string led to where the cigarette butts were once piled.

"Is that what you thought, Tony. I know I did"

"Yes, but why? They sat in their car and cleaned it and did some target practice with the van. Did they kill Frankie with the unknown weapon? Nobody around here has a gun as far as I know. The farmers have shotguns and BB guns, they don't use bullets. Did they line up the two Glens' bottles and if so why? But most importantly, who the hell are they?"

Chapter 13

Tony chose the right man for the job. The Captain wasn't a nosy neighbour just an observant one. He was a listener and an eavesdropper and people liked to talk to him. There wasn't much that was talked about that went under his radar.

For instance, at the Cream Team Cafe, while he enjoyed a cup of tea, Pearl Osborne was telling her sister Ruby how her date with Dean went.

"He brought a nice picnic and you know he's dead good looking and that. Well we were about to start kissing and we heard this crash. He goes off to investigate and so I follows him but we look and the two Glens are running, well staggering fast, up the hill. So I'm like, what do we do?, and he's like, I don't know they've run off, and I'm like yeah but what about the ice cream van, and he's like, we should just leave it."

"What ice cream van?"

"Oh yeah. Frankie Flake's van. I think the Glen's must have tried to nick it or something."

"Then what happened. With you and Dean."

"Well, I'm like do you want to go back to the sand dunes, and he's like, no I better be getting back. I mean what the hell, yeah? He's a bit weird though just talked about the moon and Easter and stuff."

"Sounds weird."

"I know, right?"

*

An old fashioned bell rang as The Captain entered the village bookshop. Dean stepped out from the bookshelves and smiled.

"Morning, Captain. How are you today?"

Good, Dean was alone.

"Fit as a fiddle and ready for love as the song says. You probably don't know that one."

"From Singing In The Rain. It's on Sky Cinema."

"Oh! You do know it. Jolly good. Listen, is my book here yet? It's been on order for some time now."

"I'll look it up for you. Dad's out shopping right now."

Dean went to the computer and tapped in the Captain's name. "It looks like it's out of print but dad has found a copy in another bookshop in Leeds. Should be here this week."

"That's fantastic news. Listen, I also wanted to ask for your expertise. I understand you like astronomy. Can you recommend a book? I really think I could make better use of my telescope. You know, point it at the sky rather than the sea, now and then. Especially at night."

Dean smiled broadly. "Yes, certainly. How did you know. Not much is secret around here I guess."

"Well that's true but I think I've seen you with your telescope on the dunes. Mainly in the winter. It's not dark enough for stargazing until long after I'm home during the summer."

"This time of year is not too bad. Some interesting skies too."

"I suppose you're a regular out there. Not as much light from the village and nearby towns if you point your telescope to the sea, eh?"

"Yes definitely."

"Last night was clear. Did you see much?"

The Captain noticed a change in Dean's demeanour. He seemed less outgoing and more like someone thinking of a bad memory.

"Dean? Are you OK?"

Dean gave a weak smile. "Yes. Let me show you some books."

"Jolly good."

They went down an aisle and Dean started showing him astronomy books. It was obviously a passion of his and the more he talked on the subject the happier he became.

"Dean, I can tell this is your passion. Your 'thing', if you will. I've had many interests and passions in my life. Sometimes it's good to share hobbies and interests but things that are real passions are best enjoyed on your own unless someone is as equally passionate as you. I loved playing chess with my officers and sometimes a passenger but when I was home I never played. My wife loved backgammon. So we played that. She loved cars and driving but to me it was just a necessary evil. She probably did more miles in her cars than I did in my ship."

"What was your joint passion?"

"Life. Each other." The Captain let that sink in then continued.

"We retired to the cottage at Lookout Point to enjoy the quiet life and fresh sea air. We enjoyed the same pursuits, good food and long walks the area offered and soon settled in to working on the cottage the way we had discussed many times in the past.

"And then, a year later, Rosemary became ill. She had never complained about anything and kept her aches and pains to herself and away from me. She said I worried about everything. Then one day she fainted and, after many days in hospital and tests and samples, the doctor gave us the sad news that she only had weeks to live.

Over the six months that followed her death, I spent all my time in the cottage fixing it up the way she had said she wanted it. I didn't care to go out and make friends with the people of Rosegarden.

When the fixing up was done, I still stayed home, moving between the bedroom, bathroom, lounge and kitchen. I phoned the grocery shop with an order and Danny would deliver it that afternoon and take payment by cheque.

I spent all my time reading, looking at old photos of me and Rosemary and I looked at her car, the Mustang that Emma May now has, and whenever it looked a little dirty I'd go and clean it.

"Then, one late afternoon on a drizzly winter's day I dozed off looking at her car and dreamt that Rosemary had packed a huge lunch basket full of my favourite food and drink. It was so heavy she couldn't lift it. I carried it to a convertible Rolls Royce I had never seen before but I knew it was ours. I turned back to get Rosemary but she just stood on the other side of the garden gate in her nightie smiling.

"'Come on love. We need to get going. All the food and drink will go off.' I said to her.

"But Rosemary laughed and said 'My silly handsome sea captain. I can't go. You have to drive off alone. Enjoy the sights and the sounds and the smells. Feel the sea breeze on your face and the sand between your toes. Remember me but go on and enjoy driving that Rolls Royce. It's full of food and I prepared it all with love. Be passionate again"

"'But I can't enjoy it without you.' I told her"

"'You can and eventually will.' She said"

"She walked back to the house and closed the door and the house disappeared.

"The next day I got in her Mustang and drove to Lands End and back. Wherever I stopped for food and fuel I talked to people and listened to them. I noticed everything around me and took in the sunset just as Rosemary and I had done so many times. I got back home in the early hours of morning and slept throughout the next day. When I woke the next morning I decided to walk into Rosegarden and talk to all my neighbours whom, so far, I hardly knew. So started my daily constitutional."

Dean noticed the trace of a tear in the Captain's eye and smiled. The Captain was one of his favourite people in the village and even more so now.

"It's always good to have someone to talk to. If you want to talk about anything I've all the time in the world."

"Like Louis Armstrong."

"Exactly. You know a lot of old songs don't you."

"I guess. That's another passion of mine you could say."

The Captain looked through one of the books Dean recommended.

"I'll take this one."

"Brilliant choice. I met the author once at a book signing."

He rang it through the till. The Captain could see he wanted to talk.

"Do you think there are many female astronomers out there, Dean?"

"I hope so. The only one I know is one of the authors I showed you and she's an old lady."
"She was your age once and I bet she was interested in the stars back then."
"I never thought of that."
After Dean popped the book in to a paper bag, The Captain held him in his gaze.
"So what happened last night?"
After the initial shock of the blunt question had gone, Dean smiled. "I was with a girl whose passion is food and not the moon or stars. Thankfully it ended when the Glens tried to steal Frankie Flake's ice cream van."
"What?"
"You must have seen it on your way in to the village."
"Yes, but I just thought an accident occurred."
"Anyway it was an excuse to get away from my date. I did come back later with my telescope. I was looking in to the Southern sky when a car pulled up in the middle of the car park."
"Really? Who was it?"
"I don't know. They were there a good while just sitting. One person was in the front smoking. I could see the orange glow. The other one got out the car and started lining up some bottles he picked from the beach. I've never seen them or their car before. Like you, I'm not good with cars so all I can say is it was dark green. I lost interest and went back home. Astronomy needs to be done without distractions."

*

The Fisherman's Arms is one of the places that strangers would probably go to when they came to Rosegarden on a Sunday. That is, of course, if they didn't just stay in their car.

The Captain sat by the window and watched the sea while waiting for his ploughman's lunch. He took a sip of bitter now and then and watched the ships far off on the horizon.

"Here we go, Captain. A ploughman's and some cutlery."

"Thanks, Steve."

"Watching the ships, eh? Do you wish you were still on them?"

"Sometimes. It's nice to be based in a quiet seaside village, though. It never gets too busy in summer either. I dare say we'll be getting visitors from this weekend on."

"Before then. We had a couple in here last night. Pair of blokes. Sort of tough looking types. Bit like Tony, you know. Nursed a pint each for over an hour. Kept looking at their watches. They hardly spoke but then only whispered when they did. They only spoke to me to order their beer and, strangest thing, to ask where Frankie Flake lives. Only they used his real name. I said I didn't know. I thought they were going to rough me up but I didn't know what they wanted and Frankie might be in trouble. Instead they left and drove off in a green car."

Chapter 14

Frankie Flake didn't fit in the freezer. Who'd have thought? Tony was surprised. It was a huge industrial freezer. He had taken out the ice cream, it would have only gone to waste now that both Frankie and his van were out of action, so he decided to donate it to the other food businesses in the village. The whippy ice cream van, or soft serve ice cream to give it its proper name, was more popular anyway. His niece, Constance, operated that, and yes, people called her Connie Cone. He had phoned her earlier to make sure she was alright. Frankie's murderer might be a serial killer with a vendetta on the ice cream trade or something. She was fine. He got her to come round and empty the ice cream from the freezer and give it away to the pubs and restaurants in the village. He told her that Frankie had gone missing. Gone off to parts unknown and there would be only her ice cream van available this year. It's what he wanted everyone to believe. He had phoned Guy Lambert to keep him up to date and asked him to relay the missing Frankie tale to the others in the council. That would be the official line for now. Lambert agreed.

But, bloody hell, Frankie Flake didn't fit in the freezer. There was still some rigour mortis, so he wasn't that flexible yet. It had been a task getting him to the freezer in the first place. After washing out Scott's vomit with a bucket of sea water, they managed to jump start the ice cream van. 'Donna a mobile' echoed out to sea and startled everyone until Tony switched it off. The diesel Emma let him have was more than enough to get them back to his large garage and storeroom he used for the ice cream vans. The next hurdle was getting Frankie's stiffened body through the doorway to the cab, over the seats and out the van. He had Mike and Paul help him and between them and a few 'to me, to you, to me, to you' they got him out and stripped and hosed him clean. Tony gave him a better inspection. The body was losing some of it's stiffness but he didn't want to wait the full forty eight hours for it to become totally supple again. There were no other visible wounds other than the small round one in his chest. What the hell was that? There was a lumpy bruise on his forehead where he must have hit the serving hatch as he fell. They patted him dry with some old rags and tried to drop him in the freezer. Instead of lying flat his shoulders and head showed above the top and he looked like he was relaxing in a deep bath.

He stood there looking down at Frankie wondering what his next step should be. "Hey Siri. What temperature are body's kept in a morgue."

"I'm sorry, I couldn't find out anything about Westminster Basement Mall."

"Oh piss off SIRI you stupid bastard."

Tony typed in the question. OK. So frozen at minus ten or chilled between two and four. Brilliant. He had just the thing.

Mike and Paul helped him clear some boxes and rubbish off the top of something under blue tarpaulin and then, like a magician delivering the big reveal, he whipped off the covers that protected the biggest delicatessen chiller his dad could afford. A beautiful Bocchini with the digital temperature readout on the back to let you know the thermostat was working. They pulled it over and plugged it in to the socket that once powered the redundant freezer.

"Alright boys, let's get him in there."

Frankie was a tall man and also broad and thick set. He fit in length ways easily but, to get him in the display, he ended up with his face and belly squashed against the glass. Usually kids with an eye on the layer cakes, colourful creamy desserts and tiramisu would press their faces against the glass from the other side.

"Yuck. Frankie looks like a specimen in a museum."

"Like a jar with body parts in?"

"Right."

"Or an animal embryo or something?"

"Right again."

"OK you two. Thanks for your help as always. Remember, this is not to be mentioned anywhere."

"Alright, boss."

"Sure no worries. It's going to be difficult chopping up pork tonight though. Let's hope nobody orders any."

Tony gave a chuckle and looked at Frankie. "Thanks, fellas. Before you go, what can you tell me about Frankie."

"Frankie only spoke to me and Paul. I don't know why, maybe because the other men were scared of his size and the women thought he was creepy or pervy. When I say spoke I mean he always said the same things and asked the same questions. Were we hitmen? Have we killed anyone? Are there any hookers nearby? Which of the local girls were easy? We just thought he was an arsehole. We pretty much ignored him and told him he had the wrong village. We never told you, nobody told you, because we thought he was full of shit and besides, he wasn't here for long. When he rocked up a couple of weeks ago I just thought, here comes that arsehole. If he carries on the way he does the boss will kick his arse out the village in double quick time."

As they left the Captain came bounding in full of jollity. Like the morning events weren't real but on TV.

"Tony! Ah, jolly good, you're still here. What's that you're looking at? Oh God! It didn't seem as bad when he was covered in ice cream. Now I'm face to face with his genitals it's a much more daunting image."

"It's not a pretty sight is it, Captain. I was just trying to figure out all that we still needed to do and who to ask what."

"Well, I can help you out there. I've been eavesdropping, questioning and listening. It looks like Frankie was often arguing with all sorts of people. Jack Dhaji saw him and Ron Greening arguing over money and Reno heard him and Charlie Osborne having a go at each other. Something about Charlie talking about Frankie to someone. Seems Frankie owed quite a few people money."

"Well there's a few motives there, I suppose."
"I also found out that Pearl from the Cream Team Cafe and Dean from the bookshop were on a picnic date on the sand dunes last night and saw the two Glens running away from the crashed ice cream van in a bandy-legged, drunken, hundred yard dash."
Tony laughed at the last bit.
"Georgia and Reno saw it too."
"I knew about the Glens but I didn't know there were witnesses."
"Yes, and Dean went back later to catch up on some star gazing but two men parked in a dark green car in the middle of the car park put him off. Seems one of them was collecting bottles from the beach and lining them up on the wall. Before that, according to Steve Grayson from the Fisherman's arms, two strangers were nursing a pint each and checking their watches. A couple of hard cases who asked where Frankie lived and called him by his real name. Jack also saw a dark car going back and forth too."
"Bloody hell! I'm not sure if I'll get anymore from Pearl and Dean. Not yet anyway. But Steve may have more about those two. Whoever they are. Captain, you're a bloody star. Great work! Come to the restaurant tonight, have a meal on me, and some vino. In the meantime I'll get Scott to meet me at Frankie's room. A couple of gangsters or hit men or hired muscle come all this way to teach Frankie a lesson. What the bloody hell did he do?

Chapter 15

	Hello Jo
Hello Guy	
	I need to ask you something. Bit of a sticky situation
I'm on holiday remember	
	How's it going
Good up until now. Mother likes Beth so that's a start. About time she accepted me.	
	Great
What do you want Guy.	
	Can you perform an autopsy?
????!!!???	
	An autopsy. On a dead person.
I'm not likely to perform one on a living person.	
	But could you.
I save, well, prolong life. My patients are all alive. Or has one died?	
	No.
Well	
	Frankie Flake. Possibly murdered.
Good God! Any suspects?	
	It's Easter this weekend.
Ah. No police in case it upsets the regulars and the villagers.	
	Exactly
Sounds like a you problem.	
	Please, Jo

What's Scott doing about this.

                    Tony's on the case.

Tony. Prime suspect number one.

                    Tony. Fixer of things.
                    Lover of Rosegarden.

FFS

                    Well

When I get back on Monday.
Make sure he's kept chilled
but not frozen.

                    Tony sorted all that.

I'll not buy dessert at his
restaurant ever again

                    Thanks' Jo

Piss off

Chapter 16

Scott had managed to lift prints off the bottles and the knife and would dust the ice cream van for prints when he got the chance. He and Tony updated each other when they met at Frankie's room. It was one of five rooms in a house Tony rented off Guy Lambert that served as digs for his staff. At least the ones who weren't family. Tony and Scott were going to question the others who lived there after they had searched Frankie's room. Not that there was much room to search. It had a single bed, a bedside table, a small chest of drawers and a chair. There was a communal dining room, kitchen and bathroom downstairs.

Under the bed they found some shoes and an empty suitcase. In the bedside table another camera and some business cards for various shops, a nightclub called Skinny Dip and escort agencies called Rendezvous, Executive Services and Discrete Meet; all in London. Despite ten years living in the capital, Tony hadn't heard of any of them. Times change, he thought, probably everything I knew has gone by now.

They searched the chest of drawers and between layers of underwear found an iPhone and iPad.

"We need to get in to these to see if there are any messages to and from those two in the pub. Trouble is we need Frankie's face and fingerprint to do so. Let's ask some questions then head back to the garage."

They searched all the pockets of his clothes and found a wallet with twenty pounds in notes, a debit card and a driving license.

"Francis Fennelli. Born October 24th 1980. That's the best ID photo I've seen. He looks almost human there."

*

Nobody knew much about Frankie. He hardly spoke to anyone and seldom used the communal areas. Especially when other people were there.

"Frankie? Who knows? That guy never spoke to nobody."

"The Flake is gone? Good riddance. That bloke never had a friend in the world and little wonder."

"Frankie? Never drank with us, or played cards or even ate with us."

"If Frankie had a friend it wasn't anyone from round here."

"Frankie only had one friend, the equally creepy Charlie Osborne."

"Frankie came back this year? I never noticed."

The females in the house always felt uneasy when he was around.

"The slimy giant? Gave me the creeps."

"The only man, resident or visitor, in the village who made me feel like I was being undressed with his eyes."

"It wasn't just us. He was always looking at the women. I saw him use his camera from his ice cream van once. I wondered what he was shooting. Then I saw Dr Jo in her bikini."

Tony shook his head and looked bewildered. "Now they tell me. I would have grilled him about all this had I known."

*

The fingerprint ID on the iPad was surprisingly easy. Tony thought Frankie's fingers may have swollen or stretched or somehow gone out of shape but the right thumb was instantly recognised. Tony put in the WiFi password and started looking through it while Scott dusted the ice cream van.

The emails all seemed to be junk with the occasional ebay notification. There were no Facebook messenger messages and nothing in Apple messages. The iPad was clearly for entertainment and nothing else. He looked at the frequently visited pages on Safari and got mainly porn sites. Looking at the history he saw escort agency listings for the nearest towns and similar enquiries for strip clubs. He closed Safari and opened the photos app. It came as no surprise when it was full of swimsuit wearing women in the photos. What was surprising was that he recognised all of them. He looked at the dates they were taken. All last summer. All women of the village and some of the tourists too. Most in bikinis, some in one pieces. There was Dr Jo. There were his nieces. There was Emma May. There was Sylvia Lambert, Guy's wife. The only one fully clothed was Maggie Marsh and she was in the background.

"Bloody hell! Frankie was a dirty bastard, Scott. I'd go so far as pervert, actually."

"Really? What you found?"

"What haven't I found. An album full of pervy pictures of the women of the village enjoying the beach. Porn sites. Escort sites and searches. Ditto strip clubs."

"Shit."

"I think we're collecting motives here. That's if the two in the green car have nothing to do with the murder."

He went back to the photos and opened another album. Posed in a farmyard was Molly Beale. The farmer's wife who was rumoured to be on very good terms with Bill Fisher. Very good terms indeed. She went from dressed in a flimsy dress to stark naked in the cowshed in eight photos.

"Looks like he had a willing poseur. Molly Beale. As in Mrs Farmer Beale. As in Bill Fisher makes lengthy stops to deliver groceries and pick up eggs there, Molly Beale."

"Really? That's three more motives perhaps."

They both looked at the photos.

"She never ages does she."

"What, Scott? Have you seen her like this before?"

"No, of course not. I meant her face and general demeanour. She has a happiness that's almost youthful that shines from within."

Tony looked at the first, fully clothed photo again.

"I see what you mean."

Tony looked at Frankie's corpse squeezed in to the chiller like he was expecting a statement from it.

"I don't really care what Molly, Bill and farmer Beale get up to, but did any of this have to do with Frankie's murder? Maybe. All I've got from the iPad was that Frankie was a pervert. Maybe his phone will be more beneficial."

Before he looked at the phone, he opened up Facebook to see who Frankie's friends were and see if he had any relatives. The only people from the village who had accepted his friend requests were Pearl and Ruby, the Selfie Sisters, as they were known. They probably just wanted another person to like their photos. There were no male friends as far as he could tell and no relatives either. He hadn't posted anything at all. The profile picture looked like he had photographed his driving licence photo.

Tony walked over to the chiller with the iPhone and tried to unlock it by pointing it at Frankie's face through the glass. It didn't work.

"Come over here and help me would you, Scott."

Scott had avoided the chiller thus far and wasn't looking forward to seeing the dead man again.

"It's alright. He doesn't look as bad now. Except he's stark bollock naked."

"Is he?"

"Well yeah. We had to clean him up. It's not as if he's going to get a chill or catch his death of cold."

"Very funny. Alright. What do you want me to do?"

"We need to twist him around and then you hold his head up while I move the phone around. Tell me as soon as it unlocks.

They jiggled Frankie's phone and head around until they got the perfect combination. The first thing Tony did was adjust the screen settings so it never turned off. The second thing was check in his notes for passwords and PIN numbers. He found a bunch of 'To Do' lists and shopping lists. There was a note with the title Passwords. That was easy, thought Tony. It was, actually, a list of passwords. They were randomly listed. Bank codes were mixed with shopping websites, passwords to apps on his phone and porn sites.

He sent himself a copy of the note.

"Any luck, Tony?"

"Yeah. Not just passwords in a note but the note wasn't locked. I'm going to check his other notes and emails now."

There was a note titled Rosegarden. It was a list of people of the village. Next to each person was a short note and a number of pound signs.

Molly Beale - photos £/ more photos or sex
Bill Fisher - Molly ££
Steve Grayson - fiddled tax ££
Guy Lambert - affair with Dr Jo £££
Sylvia Lambert - affair with Scott Hayward £££
Ross Roberts - perv. Hookers? ££
Ron Greening - old queen ££
Scott Hayward - incompetent/ bent/ queer? ££
Tony Martini - cat meat in the restaurant £
Jak Dhaji - same £
Mama Cassandra - ex porn star £ or sex

"Jesus Christ. The bastard was going to blackmail all of us. He thought I was using cat meat in the restaurant."

"Are you?"

"Don't be a twat. Of course not. He had you down as either incompetent or bent and gay. To confuse things even further you're also having an affair with Sylvia Lambert."

"The shit."

"Exactly. Well there's a few on here that may have had enough motive."

"What else is there?"

"I'm going to check his texts and email."

After a quick flick through he found all he needed.

"Looks like he asked someone down here from London because of information they would want. They asked why not just send it and he asked for cash and besides it wasn't just the information he had but a person they'd want to speak to was down here too. Someone he knew they were after."

"Any specifics? Did he say who or what he had on them?"

"No. We have no idea who the person on the other end was either."
"What about the email address?"
"It was all done by text. They never signed their name. I guess they wouldn't. Probably a burner phone. Frankie didn't want to show his hand either. He wanted them down here with cash for info. Possibly to point someone out. There's more though. At 5pm they say they're on their way and he replies to meet him at the ice cream van. They send him another at 10:23pm asking where he is and they'll meet him at eleven. He didn't answer. Then a short and to the point message 'You're dead'

Chapter 17

Tony sat in the corner booth of his restaurant and watched his staff preparing for the evening trade. The 'Reserved' plaque on the table told them he was not to be disturbed. It was unnecessary. They could see he was deep in thought. His gaze was distracted by movement but he took nothing in. He was thinking about how his day started with winning a prized Hawaiian shirt and developed in to something of a farce with him and Scott playing detectives. They didn't have a clue between them. Literally. He wasn't a policeman and in reality nor was Scott. He wore the uniform but he knew nothing of crime. It never visited Rosegarden. Not proper crime. Not jail sentence crime.

He doubted the two in the green car killed Frankie. The text they ended with was an empty psychological threat. He knew that. It's how that type operated. It's how he had operated when he was in with that type. Hunting people down that owed the boss. Threats that meant nothing, or broken limbs that meant back off. Frankie was an idiot to think they would pay him cash for information. They would have beaten it out of him then gone after whoever it was Frankie wanted to give up. And who was that? Someone on the list of potential blackmail targets? Possibly. But the two claims against him and Scott were false. Maybe the other claims were false too. He was seen arguing with Ron Greening about money. Did he actually confront him with blackmail? Nothing on the list warranted a crime boss or whoever it was to send down two enforcers, true or not.

Frankie and his list and the green car men had beckoned a dark cloud over Tony. For the last twelve years he had settled in to a peaceful and carefree existence as a well respected man of the village. As a teenager he wanted more than Rosegarden could offer and, in his early twenties, he got the excitement, nightlife and edgy experiences he craved when he lived in London for ten years and worked as an enforcer who tracked down bad clients and stray escorts from his bosses prostitution business. He was glad to leave that life behind him in the end.

But now Frankie had brought that life to Rosegarden and had a list that would upset everyone for some time to come. Could one of the men in the village be a bad client? Could one of the women be a runaway escort? He doubted either was true. There were no outsiders there. One of the men may have gone to a town, even London, for sex. It just didn't fit though.

He had told Guy Lambert about the list when he gave him an update and said that they really should bring in the police. He knew how that conversation would go, and it did.

"We're too involved now, Tony". "The list would open up a can of worms that were all lies anyway but why take a chance." "No, Dr Jo and I are not having an affair. That was ridiculous. Dr Jo is gay for starters."

He and Scott were interviewing people of the town tomorrow, The Fisherman's Arms would be their first stop. Hopefully Steve Grayson took down the license plate of the green car.

It already seemed obvious to Tony. To see why they came to Rosegarden, he would have to go to them, even if it meant crawling among the lowlife of some town or city's underworld.

*

The restaurant was fairly busy for a Monday evening. The Captain was there early to take Tony up on his offer and they ate together. Emma had already messaged him to say that she would eat with him at the restaurant on Wednesday if that was ok. Of course it was. He thought he could really do with some female company tonight, but maybe by Wednesday they'd be celebrating or he'd need her company even more.

The Captain was good company though. Tony imagined it was after all those cruises where, as part of the job, he had to host evening meals at his table.

"You can tell how good an Italian restaurant is by the smell." declared the Captain.

"Really? You mean the amount of garlic or herbs or something?"

"Not quite. A basic, OK, Italian restaurant will smell nice but a great Italian restaurant will make your mouth water and almost make you float, cartoon like, to your table."

Tony laughed imagining the Captain as a cartoon figure going dreamy eyed and floating to his table.

"And how does mine rate in the nostrils?"

"I'm still floating."

"Hah! Thank you. I have great chefs and kitchen staff."

"You chose them and hired them. The only people allowed to move to the village without Guy Lambert and the council's say-so."

"So was Frankie Flake and he turned out to be not that great."

Tony gave him the rundown of what he had found out about Frankie so far including the blackmail list.

"That's a lot of bad in one person. Hm. Let's think about this in chunks."

"OK. Tell me what you're thinking."

"Firstly, nobody really knew him. You gave him the job because Alfredo recommended him, and that was because they were each other's only relative. That also means that Frankie didn't know anybody."

The Captain took a sip of red wine, smiled and took a bigger sip.

"Nice wine, Tony.

"Anyway, back to Frankie. Secondly, he never spoke to anyone except two people he thought were hitmen in disguise. But he must of also talked to, or tried to talk to some of the women because they all agree he said unpleasant things to them, or at least uncomfortable things. All are unanimous in their repulsion of him. He must have also spoken to customers buying ice cream and also Charlie Osborne"

"I'm not sure what you're getting at, Captain."

"Well, just that, someone must have gossiped about the things on the list. Unless he made it all up. We know that two things on the list are true. Both to do with Molly. Does that mean that Molly is the person with the gossip? Maybe. But the Molly/ Bill Fisher affair is common gossip he could have picked up from anywhere. Ron Greening is gay. Nobody bothers about anything like that anymore but, Frankie may have found out and pushed him for gossip."

"Why would Ron give it up though. Nobody cares who is and isn't gay. This isn't the eighties."

"True, but maybe Frankie found it out and tempted him with sex."

Tony gave this some thought while their meals were served.

"I doubt that's a scenario but when we question Ron we maybe able to fish some facts out."

"Here's another thing. When he asked about easy women or hookers in the area and even searched the same thing on the internet, was that for his needs or was he actually looking for a particular person? Someone he knew lived in this area."

Tony stopped chewing for a moment then swallowed and sipped on his beer.

"Very good question. But nobody around here fits that description. At least not in the village."

"You don't know what goes on behind drawn curtains. Or what happens when someone visits town or spends the week, supposedly, visiting with relatives. Dr Jo says she's visiting relatives with Beth until Thursday and we have no reason to doubt her, but, how many others have gone away? Some, like Jerry Wade, go away every month."

"Does he?"

"Yes. He's a re-enactment man. Never understood it myself. Also some people go regularly to listen to live music we don't get around here. Lots of reasons to regularly go away, really. What I'm saying is that anyone could live a part time double life away from here if they wanted."

"I see what you mean."

"Another thing about Frankie is that, as far as we know, he hasn't ventured out of the village. Not this year anyway. So I would think his murderer is someone who lives in the village, or visits it, and somebody he's threatened with blackmail or pestered too much."

"I would say somebody who lives in the village as nobody, except delivery men, have visited. Not to my knowledge, anyway. The farmers and their wives are too busy this time of year and I've not seen Farmer Beale or Molly around here."

"Yes, I suppose Daisy hasn't barked at passing cars much this year. So what now?"

Tony ate the last bit of broccoli and walnut panzanella, took a swig of beer and wiped his mouth, with a look of deep concentration from start to finish.

"All we can do now," he said, "is question the people in the village after that and then I'll go and see whoever owns that green car. You can carry on doing what you do and get some more information. Tomorrow, you, me and Scott split up and sweep the village with questions. I just can't imagine anyone from the village having a dark secret and I certainly can't picture any of them killing."

"Who's first on your list?"

"Charlie Osborne. He's a pervy bloke and so was Frankie. People with things in common chat and compare notes. Some we've questioned say those two were friends. I'm interested what he has to say."

Chapter 18

The next morning the temperature had dropped by a couple of degrees and the breeze had picked up by a couple of knots but that didn't stop Tony from wearing his regulation Hawaiian shirt over a white tee and chinos. Scott was in his uniform as usual.
"Nice shirt, Tony. Hawaiian as usual but quite subdued colours. Browns and golden browns and white. I'd wear that. If I ever get out of this uniform that is."
"My shirts are never crazy loud and never tacky."
"Maybe not for you but for a law enforcement officer they are."
"I won't take offence. Right, down to business, first port of call Charlie   Osborne."

There had always been a tourist shop where Caught In A Dream now stood. Originally it was called Beside The Seaside and then Kiss Me Quick followed by The Bucket And Spade then Fudge And Saucy Cards until Charlie Osborne's father, Dave, settled on the present name inspired by all the dream catchers they sold. Nobody could explain why dream catchers, incense and CDs of whale music should be stocked in a seaside tourist shop apart from the fact that they sold as well as the packaged fudge, tea towels and postcards that featured Rosegarden's street scenes and sea views. But they did. The other surprising thing about the shop was that, despite all the names it had gone through, there had only been three people who had managed it, Charlie Osborne, Dave Osborne and his father Gilbert. Dave and Gilbert were the ones who tried different things and names and kept the village happy with the family orientated stock. There had always been local postcards and prints of resident artist Ross Roberts's landscapes. Ross had his own shop and gallery a couple of doors down that sold a wider range of art as well as original oils and watercolours.

Guy Lambert had raised concerns in the last full meeting of last year that Caught In A Dream had a smaller turnover and much smaller profit that summer than any other year. "Don't worry," Charlie Osborne had assured him, "things are on course to be the biggest year next year. Especially with my new stock. And possibly a name change."

Tony and Scott's entrance was announced by a tinkling bell. Charlie was nowhere in sight. They looked around at the new stock. The boxed fudge, incense, relaxation CDs, paintings by local artists, and classy photographic postcards had given way to penis shaped red candy, postcards of bikini wearing women on beaches nowhere near Rosegarden, little figurines of naked fat men bent over with anuses that doubled as pencil sharpeners, anatomically correct replicas of male and female genitals made of pewter that could be used as paperweights, doorstops or just ornaments. Novelty ties depicting huge breasted women in thongs and high heels hung side by side with aprons that made the wearer look like a muscle man, naked except for a posing pouch. Nearer to the back, on high shelves were girlie magazines and pornographic DVDs.

The only things kept in stock since the days of Dave were the sticks of rock, the bucket and spade sets and the little windmills on sticks.

Charlie came in from behind a curtain in the back of the shop wiping his hands, slightly out of breath and a little sweaty.

"Pardon us if we don't shake your hand, Charlie." Tony said with obvious disdain.

"Well, well, well! The Starsky and Hutch of Rosegarden. Or should that be Poirot and Hastings? Or even Cagney and Lacey?"

Scott frowned, Tony laughed. "It's Sergeant Hayward and Mr Martini to you, Osborne."

"Of course. Any time, any place, anywhere, here's Martini."

Scott frowned, Tony laughed and then stepped forward and grabbed Charlie Osborne by the seaside saucy novelty tie and pulled downwards then led him to the front of the shop and with the other hand flipped the sign to closed and locked the door and then led him to the cash desk and pulled down further on the tie until the shopkeeper's forehead was on the counter and his purple face dangled over the edge. With a couple of hard yanks Osborne's head bashed against the edge.

"Right. Shall we start again. Good morning, Charlie. Sergeant Hayward and I need to ask you about the disappearance of Francis Fennelli, known to everybody as Frankie Flake."

He let go of the tie and Osborne came up gasping. "Jesus fucking Christ, Tony. I was only messing around." He caught his breath. "I thought Frankie was killed. I saw the photos. You were there, Scott, at the meeting, you saw."

"The official line, as Guy would have told you, is that he disappeared after wrecking the ice cream van."

"Yeah, he did say that. I thought he was joking though."

"That's your problem, Charlie, you think everyone is joking and everything is a joke." Tony looked around the shop. "Do you know what really hit my buttons? Looking at the state of this place. What the hell have you done? It used to be a classy tourist shop. Now it's like some tacky shit place in Blackpool or Southend or something."

"It was boring. All those Dream Catchers and Song of the Whale CDs. What does that hippy crap have to do with the seaside?"

"Alright what about the local artists section and the classy postcards? The boxes of fudge with photos of the Rosegarden on the front. It's all tat now." Scott was getting animated on the subject.

"I fell out with Ross Roberts. He wouldn't paint what I wanted him to."

"Ross has standards. I can imagine what you wanted paintings of you smutty creep."

"Never mind about all that" Tony brought it back to the questions about Frankie. "When did you last see Frankie?"

"Saturday night. We had a pint at the Fisherman's."

"What did you talk about?"

"Just catching up type stuff. What he'd been up to in London. Why he decided to come back here even though he hated it. And he hated you, Tony. He said you were all mouth and show and just a pussy in a flowery shirt. His words not mine."

"Glad you made that clear. Go on."

"He said he'd make money this year. Real money."

"Really? How?"

"He didn't give details. Just said he knew things that would make him a pile. Just had to pretend to be an ice cream man for another month or so then leave here forever."

"Come on Charlie. Don't dick us around. He must have said something."

"Just that everyone has secrets and he knew all of them."

"Did he get that from you?"

"No, Mr Martini. Honest."

"Seeing as he never spoke to anyone but you I find that hard to believe."

"Maybe he did. Speak to others that is."

"What about Molly?" Scott asked. "Molly Beale?"

Charlie Osborne looked nervous and shifty.

"What about her?" he asked. "She's a tart."

"Be nice, Charlie or I may have another look at your lovely tie."

Osborne involuntarily adjusted his tie.

"Now answer Sergeant Hayward's question. Did Frankie ever mention Molly?"

"He bragged he banged her but I didn't believe him."

"Why not? You called her a tart a moment ago."

"Well, Tony, he just seemed full of shit and always on the prowl and perving after women."

"He must of loved it in here then. He found a kindred spirit with you, didn't he?"

Osborne shuffled from foot to foot and looked at the floor. "This stuff sells."

"Really? Then how come you have a stack of five year old nude calendars in the corner over there?"

"Oh and what are these?" Scott was at the back of the shop. "Barbecue sets?

I hope you tell the people who buy these they're not allowed on the beach or in any of the grounds in Rosegarden? Look at these skewers, Tony. One of these could be a strong contender for our murder weapon."

"Here hang on. I never killed Frankie. I never killed anyone."

"Scott has a point though, Charlie. A metal skewer like that could be our murder weapon. Maybe you sold it to the murderer if you didn't do it yourself."

"I've not sold any since last year. And yes I did make it clear that the barbecue sets were not to be used around here."

Scott nodded. "OK, Charlie. Apart from the dodgy barbecue sets, does Guy know you sell these and all the smut? He wants this to be a quaint old fashioned seaside village, not a miniature Blackpool."

"Guy doesn't care. When was the last time he came in here? People pretend to care but they don't. You don't, Tony. You go about looking busy but you're ignoring everyone and everything. Trying to hide your past, Tony?"

"Keep talking like that and you won't have a future."

"That's it, Tony, just like your old days. Maybe you killed Frankie."

Tony connected the heel of his hand with Charlie's chin. It was quick and hard and brutal. His head snapped back then forward then back to its original position and Charlie had tears in his eyes.

Everyone paused and caught their breath. Scott looked frightened.

"Tell you what, Charlie. Answer mine and Sergeant Hayward's questions and we'll let you slowly change your shop back to how it was. If you don't want to sell dream catchers, ok, don't. Just change the shop's name to something suitable like The Bucket and Spade. Guy won't mind that. He will close you down if he sees how far you've slid down the greasy sleaze pole though. Understand?"

Charlie nodded and sniffed.

Tony gave him a warm smile. "OK. Now tell me how you and Frankie became drinking buddies. What you really talk about and why Molly got with Frankie. No dicking around."

Charlie walked to the back of the shop. The other two followed him past the barbecue sets and through a multi coloured tassel door curtain that Tony remembered from his childhood.

Charlie sat down at a small kitchen table that was topped with boxes of stock. "Sit down and let me tell you about Frankie."

They sat down and waited while he chose his words.

"When Frankie came here last summer it wasn't his first visit to Rosegarden. He visited his uncle when we were both in our early teens and we met in this shop. We hit it off and spent all his time here together. He only stayed a couple of nights with his uncle and then went back traveling around. We kept in contact. We both like the ladies. Well we liked sex and we liked to see what we could, if you know what I mean."

"No, I don't." Tony said. "Do you, Scott?"

"No."

"You know. Cleavage here, panty line there, cheek hanging out. Nice bum in tight trousers. That sort of thing."

Tony shook his head. "Go on."

"Well, we always sent each other photos. We'd delete the messages but keep the photos. He used to send loads from London. I used to send him pictures of the women on the beach here."

Tony and Scott looked at each other.

"Then when he came back last summer it sort of dried up. He didn't get many good pics from his van and it was all one way. I told him it didn't matter. After his stint selling ice cream he'd be back in London. He said he'd seen plenty of women he didn't get pics of who went past the RG scale. But.."

"The what?"

"I'm guessing, Scott, that Charlie and Frankie rated women to some sort of scale based on the women around here."

Charlie looked awkward and didn't know where to look or put his hands.

"Well yeah. Maggie was the bottom of the scale and Molly was the top. It was based on sexiness rather than pure looks."

"I don't want to know more about your grubby rating system. Alright? Now, how did he act when he got back this year?"

"Funny you should ask, but he was low when he got back. He said he'd seen and screwed really good looking women in London and this place was a shit hole with no women. Then said he had a plan to make some money. He asked me for information but there's nothing going on around here so I made a load of stuff up. I thought if he went through with his blackmail plan, it would fall through anyway because it was all crap."

"You mean like my restaurant serving up cat meat?"

"What? How did you know about that?"

"Same way I found all those photos of your RG scale."

Charlie slumped in his chair and stared in to space.

"Did you take those photos of Molly?"

Charlie nodded.

"So all the things on his list came from you?"

Charlie nodded.

"I wanted Ross Roberts to paint the nudes of Molly for me. I offered him quite a bit. But he didn't want anything to do with it."

"Never mind that. Tell me about the blackmail."

He was going to wait until July and spring it on everyone. Thing is, when I saw him on Saturday, he said bollocks to the list he had something much bigger in the works. He wouldn't say what, but he was going to meet some London types. He said they would pay him for information. Apparently the person he had the info on wouldn't pay up and so he called them to come down. I don't know if they did or not."

"Is that why you and Frankie argued the other day?"

"What? We never argued."

"That's not what I heard."

"Well, we argued but I was telling him not to call anybody. It would bring grief to the village"

"Who was he phoning? About whom?" Scott was getting louder.

"I don't know and I don't know. Not you if that's what you're getting so excited about." Charlie laughed "I wondered when the official policeman was going to ask something" Scott's fist connected with his sweaty cheek. Tony got between them. "Alright Scott. Don't lower yourself to slapping this buffoon around.

"Now, Charlie, how did you get Molly to pose for you?"

"She's a tart who loves attention and never gets any from her husband. All I had to do was say it was for an artist to paint her. It was easy. Silly bitch."

Charlie laughed and, as always seemed to happen, he laughed alone.

"Pack your bags, Osborne. As soon as Guy hears what a total sleaze bag you are he'll close you down and I'll be there to help him."

"Fuck you, Martini. I hope those Londoners are after you."

"Maybe they are, Osborne. Maybe they are."

Chapter 19

"Nothing Charlie said is a hundred per cent believable. Possible perhaps, but most of it seems off. Molly maybe fun and confident but I doubt she let that sleaze bag photograph her stripping off. We ought to lock him up just for being sleazy."

Scott thought about Tony's words as they approached The Fisherman's Arms. "Well, yes but, as a police officer I have to be impartial and anti vigilante. That said, he is a sleaze bag and I'm glad he may be gone soon."

They knocked on the door and rang the bell of the pub. It wasn't any use getting there before Steve Grayson had his pot of coffee and hair of the dog. He wasn't that responsive until his second or third lunchtime pint, to be fair.

"Morning lads." His bleary eyes came a little to life.

"Morning, Steve. Alright if Tony and I ask you a few questions about Sunday night."

"Oh about those two blokes? The Captain must have told you what I said."

"Yeah, he spoke to me about it." Tony replied.

"Scary buggers they were. Like your two, Tony. No chefs though. Just thugs.

Look, come on in and we'll chat."

They followed Steve in to the pub that still smelled of last nights beer and the curious odour of upholstery that were as much a part of any pub as the sign outside. They stood by the bar.

"Those two asked about Frankie. Where he lived and where was he. I could have told him but I was fearful for the others who lived in the house."

Steve paused, got behind the bar and poured himself a pint of local ale. "Fancy one fellas?"

It was ten o'clock.

"Not while I'm on duty, thanks, Steve."

"Bit early for me thanks."

"Oh, thanks for the ice cream by the way, Tony."

"No problem. Now Frankie's disappeared and the van's out of action it would just go to waste."

"Missing is he? Be those two from Sunday I reckon."

"That's what we think too." Tony said. "Can you give us details about them? What they looked like, what they drank, did they go out to smoke, did they make any phone calls? Anything."

"Well let's see now. They both drank pints. One had local ale." Steve held up his half finished pint. "This stuff. The other spring water. Both nursed their pints too. Imagine. A pint of spring water. Neither spoke on the phone and only whispered to each other now and then. One kept tidying everything around him. The one with the spring water. The beer mats, the glasses, their phones. I don't think I saw them go out for a smoke but the other one, the one who didn't tidy all the time, was the one who asked about Frankie and he smelled strongly of cigarettes. They seemed annoyed and kept looking at their watches and I'm sure they glanced at the bar clock now and then."

"Anything else?"

"When they left. Mr Tidy told me that, if I see Frankie let him know he wasn't welcome in London anymore and he would understand. Then they got in their car and drove off. I wrote down the licence plate. A dark green Vauxhall Insignia. Here it is Sarge"

Steve took a beer mat from between the till and the counter and handed it to Scott.

"That's great, Steve, thanks."

"How about descriptions?"

"Well Mr Tidy was over six foot tall and looked like he spent most of his spare time in the gym. The other was a six footer too though not as tall. Thick set. Old school hard man type. They both wore business casual. No visible tattoos but Mr Tidy's mate had a big gold earring in his right ear."

Scott looked up from his notebook. "Any accents?"

"Maybe London, or Essex or Kent. Who knows."

"Tell us what you know about Frankie."

"Not much to tell, Tony. He seldom came in here and when he did he sat in the corner and watched everyone over his pint. No matter how much fun was going on or what was being talked about, he never joined in. He never even changed the expression on his face, never laughed or even cracked a smile. Weird bloke. Tell a lie. I seen him come to life once. Molly and her sister came in. It was hot and, well you know Molly, she wasn't wearing a lot. He followed her round the room with his eyes and when she looked over at him he smiled. When they left he followed them."

"Do you know what happened after that?"

"Yes Sarge. Nothing. Well nothing happened to Molly. Bill Fisher was here as well. He followed her and her sister out too. There were a few words spoken between the two men but no fisticuffs."

It wasn't much that they didn't already know, apart from the car registration and the Bill Fisher confrontation.

"Thanks, Steve. If you think of anything else let us know."

"Will do, Tony."

Tony and Scott went outside. Steve pulled his second pint.

"A bit more info, Tony."

"Yes. Let's meet up with the Captain and split the rest of the questioning between us. I'm sure we'll get closer."

"Let's hope so. Who knows who else may get killed."

Chapter 20

The Captain met Tony on the seafront outside the Gutty Shark. He had Daisy with him. Daisy's nose was going left and right and round in circles. Now and then she licked her lips.
"Maybe we'll get you a sausage after we've asked our questions, old girl.
Tony laughed. "I don't think we'll have to sniff for clues, Captain."
"That's a pity. No, I didn't want to leave her alone all day again and she's an ice breaker when I need to start a conversation. You know something, I just remembered Frankie once told me he wished he had a dog because it was a great conversation starter. Especially with the women. I'm not one to speak ill of the dead, but, I'm not sure if he was awkward, lonely, creepy or a real swine."
"Maybe we'll find out today, Captain. I'll start at the top of the hill and work my way down. You concentrate on the shops, restaurants and the hotel. I want to interview Maggie though, you've already been there. When Scott gets back he can question the trades people. I doubt if Frankie spoke to any of them but you never know."
"Where is Scott?"
"He's back at the station house making phone calls to find out more about the dark green car. I'm keen to know more about that. Probably be more useful than our questions today. You never know, though. Someone may have important info."

*

There were only a couple of couples having a cream tea in the Cream Team Cafe. Pearl was wiping the shelves behind the counter and Ruby was tidying up the back area. Maggie must be in. Or The Immaculate Convention as some people called her. Everything was squeaky clean and she spent most of her spare time knitting or walking on the beach or hiking around the surrounding farmland. Always plainly dressed in almost frumpy styles, no one had seen her in the Fisherman's or the Crow's Nest. She bought the same food every week from the local shops including tuna for the cat. She was always smiling though. The smile of someone who was at least twenty years her senior. At first Tony thought it was a stage smile but it was still there when she was outside the cafe. She seemed very happy with life. The first time she seemed less than happy was just now, when he asked about Frankie. She frowned and looked out the window to the sea.

"Those photos I saw were awful. I never liked him but nobody deserves to end up like that."

"Why didn't you like him?" Tony knew the answer but asked anyway.

"Well nobody likes to speak ill of the dead, but he was a pervert. I saw him take photos with that little camera. I looked towards what he was photographing. Turned out to be Emma May in her bikini. Then I saw him snap others. I went to his van and he gave me such a leer. Me. I never dress provocatively. Not that it should matter. Men shouldn't leer that way. He asked me if I wanted something to lick or suck. I walked away and left him standing there. He was probably laughing."

"I'm so sorry, Maggie. I'm only finding out what he was like since he went missing. If I had known he wouldn't have been allowed back. I should have checked up on him and asked."

"It's not your fault."

"I have to disagree." After a pause he continued, "Did he ever come in here?"

"No. Thank God."

"Can I ask the sisters some questions?"

"Yes. Of course."

*

"Yeah. He asked to be our Facebook friend. I knew he was a bit pervy but a like is a like and he liked everything we posted."

"Yeah. I think he liked Ruby more though. She's got a better figure."

"Nothing wrong with yours babe."

"Did he ever cross the line?"

"What line?" Pearl wanted to know.

"You know, babe, imaginary line, yeah. Like saying the wrong thing."

Pearl thought about it and said, "Yeah. That one time. I'm like, you like my pics don't you? And he's like, yeah, got any nudie ones? And I'm like, I'm not like that. I told him where to go."

"Was that when we stopped talking to him, babe?"

"Yeah. Perv."

"Did you ever hear anyone threaten him or tell him to leave town? I only ask because you're on that end of the beach a lot."

Both girls thought about it.

"Ross Roberts used to get angry with him and told him he brought the tone down."

"Yeah, I remember that." said Pearl. "It was the end of last summer, just before Frankie left."

Tony looked at the Ross Roberts paintings that adorned the cafe walls.

"I can't imagine him getting angry."

"Nor can I." Agreed Maggie who had joined them. "Such a sweet and gentle man. He loves this village and the countryside around it. He fell out with that other creepy man, Charlie Osborne, as well. He really disliked how they lowered the tone of the village."

Chapter 21

The only road that went into Rosegarden terminated at the western end of it. At the conclusion of the road, a small precinct of art deco commercial buildings nestled into the hillside. The first door welcomed the visitors to an antique shop called Old and Glorious. Daisy drank from the bowl of water outside the door and then she and the Captain walked in.

A bell tinkled and the noise lingered a little too long before fading in to silence. Even then the Captain thought it could still be heard.

"Won't be a moment". The voice came from somewhere deep in the back of the shop.

"Hello Captain! And Daisy, also. Can I give her a treat Captain."

Daisy wagged her tail.

"I can't see why not, Ahmed."

"Hey, Fatima, bring out a treat for Daisy."

Fatima and their son Yusuf rushed between the rows of antiques and collectibles with a treat for Daisy.

"Gently now Yusuf, don't frighten Daisy."

"You too, Daisy. Sit and take the treat nicely."

Daisy did as the Captain said then licked Yusuf's hand after swallowing the treat whole. "Good girl, Daisy"

"Come on back now Yusuf, let dad and the Captain talk."

"Bye Captain Nightingale. Bye Daisy."

"Bye Yusuf. That's a fine lad you have there, Ahmed." The Captain said after the boy had gone.

"Yes, I'm lucky. So, Captain, how is your telescope? You on another shopping trip?"

"It's amazing. I'm always astounded by how an antique like that creates such a clear and bright image. The mechanics are wonderful too. I will have a browse today but I'm actually here asking about a strange occurrence."

"Oh? What's happened?"

"Frankie Flake ruined his van then disappeared. Happened Sunday night."

"The van was serving ice cream at night?"

"No. But he appears to have disappeared that night. Did you hear or see anything unusual?"

"Not on Sunday night. Saturday morning, Frankie asked me if we sold guns."

"Good grief, did he?"

"Yes. Not to fire it, he said. Just to make people believe he had a gun that he could use to defend himself. I told him we only have 17th century muskets and never get guns in because it goes against Rosegarden's values."

"What did he say to that?"

"Said we were all sanctimonious arseholes. I laughed in his face. He called me an offensive name, turned around and walked off. That's the last I saw of him."

"How did he seem?"

"A little crazy, a little nervous too."

The Captain had a browse around then walked out empty handed but, after a good look around, realised that the shop was full of potential weapons, and, with Ahmed's relaxed attitude, anyone could shoplift one.

Chapter 22

If Rosegarden looked like rows of theatre seats descending down the hill, then Ross Roberts had one of the royal boxes. From his house he could see all the rooftops, most of the beach and a large part of the rose garden at the top of the hill. The view of the sea inspired him everyday and gave him a sense of inner peace and greater chi. Being unburdened by the responsibilities of running a village that his cousin felt daily, his only torment was what to paint and when. There was so much beauty everywhere and so much, literally, on his doorstep. Some days he would hike amongst the farmland or walk along the coast to sketch or paint or photograph landscapes to use later, for light is always changing and is seldom the same twice. He often painted portraits of the people of the village for his own pleasure or for a commission or as gifts and sometimes touristy landscapes to hang in the restaurants and pubs or sell in his shop and Caught In A Dream, although that repugnant man who had taken over the shop wanted nudes and bikini girls. He had given the creepy sweaty oaf a piece of his mind and demanded he reinstate the landscapes and seascapes the tourists loved. If it was the same by the Easter weekend his cousin would be brought in to the argument. But for now it was best to ignore all negativity and concentrate on the good vibes the earth emitted so strongly around their village.

After Easter he would have to start planning for all the ceramic roses to be collected and cleaned and stored in June, until later in the year when he'd get any that needed it, repaired or repainted by the school children. He'd have to ask the school to retrain staff and pupils about health and safety. Last year two children and Sonia Dhaji hurt themselves on the sharp points of the metal stems.

He stood on the front terrace and watched the village and the sea that he had spent the morning sketching. He was about to stop for lunch when he saw Tony appear.

"Ah, Tony. Always nice to see you. Can I get you some tea or my own homemade lemonade."

"A tank of oxygen and a mask might be better. I hardly ever come up here and I always forget how steep the top part is. Good excuse to join the Captain for a portion of chips later."

"Ha! Yes it is quite steep on the last bit. Come in and sit down. I'll get that lemonade and let you catch your breath."

Tony sat down at the table by the window and looked at a ship on the distant horizon.

"It really is a pretty view here."

"Yes. Inspirational" Shouted Ross from the kitchen and then came out with a heavy ceramic pitcher and matching beakers.

They settled down with their drinks and Ross asked, "So, Tony, did you come all the way up here for the view or to get your portrait painted? I would love to paint you. You have a strong face and a good head of hair going grey at the temples. A characteristic aquiline nose and dark brown eyes that, if I painted them correctly, would see through the people looking at the canvas."

"Thank you. I think. I'll bear that in mind. Anyway." he took a drink of the lemonade. "Delicious."

"Thank you. You were saying."

"Yes. I actually made it up the hill to ask you about Frankie Flake."

"Oh God, no. Not that swine. Has he returned? I thought you would have given him the boot."

"Unfortunately I only found out about the, erm, less savoury side of him, since he returned and then disappeared."

He watched Ross Roberts closely. Was there a slight pause or flicker. Some recognition of something. He thought so but wasn't sure.

"Disappeared eh? Can't say I'll miss him."

"So you haven't seen him this year."

"No. I confronted him last year because of his foul behaviour. He even picked on poor Maggie. Not many people see me lose my temper but he brought it out in me."

"As did Charlie Osborne?"

Ross looked shocked.

"Well yes." He took a sip of his lemonade to gather his thoughts. "I wondered why he hadn't requested any new landscapes from me and went to his shop. I was horrified by what he had done. To make matters worse Frankie was in there. They both thought it was hilarious for me to react the way I did. And he later had the nerve to ask me to paint various women of the village and some anonymous tourists from photos they had taken on the beach. All in their swimsuits. To top it all he produced photos of Molly Beale. From half dressed to totally naked. I practically threw him down the hill."

"I see. So you haven't seen Frankie this year?"

"No. Definitely not."

They both sipped their lemonades

"On a brighter note, would you paint a group portrait of me and my staff. Maybe a couple of landscapes too."

"I have some landscapes in my studio. Come with me. Have a look."

They walked through the house and up an outside staircase that led to an upper terrace with a large shed in one corner. Tony followed Ross inside.

"Here are the landscapes. Oh. Here is one painted from the hill on the other side. You can see your restaurant."

"Wonderful. I'll take that one." Tony looked round and saw several portraits of the people of the village and the farmers too. One side of the studio looked like Ross's tool and paint area. Plenty of pallet knives but nothing long and cylindrical and thin and sharp.

"The portraits are excellent."

"Thank you."

For the first time Ross seemed slightly embarrassed. Then Tony noticed why. Half the portraits were of Maggie."

"Maggie is my muse. Nothing sordid of course. As you can see."

"It's Maggie as we all see her. Walking, working and knitting. They are very good."

"Thanks."

Tony looked closer at the Maggie portraits and the knitting one caught his eye.

"Crikey. Those are big knitting needles. Are they really that big or did you use artistic license?

"They really are that big. Maggie uses large ones for thick knit cable stitch sweaters."

"Does she really? Oh those sweaters that the local craft shop sells."

"Those are the ones. Have one myself. Caught In A Dream used to sell them too."

Tony kept looking at the paintings.

"Did you have any more questions, Tony. I hate to seem rude but I haven't had lunch yet and I have a private study pupil coming here after lunch."

"Oh apologies, Ross. Also apologies for not getting rid of Frankie last year."

"Not at all, Tony. Not at all. Let's hope he never comes back."

Tony walked back down the hill and thought about a new question. Could a knitting needle, like the ones in Ross's portrait of Maggie, be used to kill a man?

Chapter 23

Fred Ling had just cut his brother, Lee's hair and was settling in the chair for his trim when the Captain and Daisy walked in. He started to get out the chair.

"No please stay seated and get your hair trimmed, Lee."

"I'm Fred, he's Lee. What's the matter Cap? We all look the same to you?"

"Only you two. You are identical twins after all."

This was one of those exchanges that happened every time they met. Always instigated by Fred while Lee smiled in the background, quietly watching. The Captain didn't mind, in fact, it was one of those regular things that made you feel as though everything was OK and as it should be. Lee will now ask if Daisy or the Captain want a trim.

"Ok Cap. Who's in the seat next though, you or Daisy."

"Neither, today" the Captain said, "I just wanted to ask you about Frankie Flake. He seems to have disappeared."

"Oh man, that's too bad. We're going to miss him asking us to teach him Kung Fu or Karate. He thought we were a double Bruce Lee or Jackie Chan or something. Especially last time we saw him. He wanted self defence lessons. Said he may need it soon."

"Did he say why? When was this?"

"Saturday morning first thing. Came in for a haircut and did the whole Chinese stereotype thing. Said someone may be looking to get him."

"Yeah we thought it was bullshit. Some bragging to back up the racism." This was the first time Lee had spoken.

"See. Lee is so pissed off he chose to speak. The only Chinese thing we do is Tai Chi, as you know Cap. Don't forget tonight on the beach at seven. Daisy can come too."

"Yes we will be there, won't we old girl?"

Daisy wagged her tail and went over to Lee and laid on her back.

"You floozy, Daisy." Lee said rubbing her belly.

"My God, Lee, two sentences in one day."
The Captain laughed and called Daisy. Walking out the shop he wondered if anyone would have anything good to say about Frankie and who was he frightened of.

Chapter 24

Behind the Village Hall and facing the hill are all the trades' workshops and stores, neatly in a row and named by signs with the original artwork from the 1930's when it was realised that the beautiful village would need maintaining. A small team of plumbers, carpenters, painters, locksmiths, electricians, gardeners and builders all start their day there. They also go back there for their tea breaks and lunch for free meals and drinks.

Scott got to the canteen at lunchtime and decided to address everyone all at once.

"Hello everyone. I'm here on official business."

"Oh dear, has someone been rearranging the ceramic roses again?" Someone shouted out.

Here we go, thought Scott, all aboard the banter bus.

"I know, I know, we don't get much crime here in Rosegarden but Frankie Flake has disappeared and his van was found to be tampered with on Monday morning."

Everyone started speaking at once.

"Does anyone know anything about Frankie that seems odd?" Scott said above the noise and as soon as he did he knew it wasn't the right thing to ask.

When the laughter subsided and the quips died down, Scott tried another tact.

"We'll if anyone wants to talk to me about Frankie after lunch I'll be over here."

When lunches were over, the men and women filed past him and smiled apologetically until the only person left in the canteen apart from him was an electrician called Barbara.

"I can't stop long, Scott, I've got a job on at the Village Hall this afternoon, I just wanted to tell you about Frankie."

"That's great" Scott said getting out his notebook. "What can you tell me?"

"We'll he isn't a great person, as you probably know, but he isn't as bad as others say. Most of the stuff he says is awkward, clumsy and stupid but he doesn't know what else to say or how to act. Sometimes he says things to shock and be funny. He's never offended me because I know how to take him."

"OK, Barbara, that's good to know. When was the last time you saw him?"

"On Sunday afternoon. About three. I finished early and decided to get an ice cream. I prefer real ice cream to that Mr Whippy stuff. We have a little banter, you know, give me a kiss and I'll give you free ice cream. I always answer that he doesn't have enough ice cream. We laugh and that is that."

"Did he say anything else? How was he? What sort of mood was he in?"

"He said nothing about going away although he did say that coming back was a mistake. Thinking about it, he did seem a little more downbeat than usual. I never noticed before."

"How so?"

"Well, he said the kiss for an ice cream thing, but it was like he was playing a part. Come to think of it, he practically rushed the transaction and never looked me in the eye. I guess, I'm so used to his banter, I imagined it happened."

"So he was distracted?"

"Yes. But like I said, I didn't really notice it."

"Do you know what Frankie does in his down time? Who, if anyone, he knocks around with?"

"Well, we don't talk about that much, but I know he is friends with Charlie Osborne. He is the real perv. Frankie is only bad when they're together. Charlie is bad all the time. I heard that Charlie sees hookers in London when he goes away in the winter. I wouldn't be surprised if he talked Frankie in to going too."

Scott stopped writing and stared at Barbara for a moment.

"Barbara, that's not something I've heard before. You have a higher opinion of Frankie than the majority of people in the village."

"That's because nobody knows how to listen. I wanted to know why he is like he is. So I listened. He deserves to be in Rosegarden more than Charlie. Charlie is hear just because his parents and grandparents are from here. He's done nothing to deserve living here.

"Maybe Frankie's gone off to find somewhere more accepting."

All Scott could think of, was Charlie visited prostitutes.

Chapter 25

Ron Greening lived halfway up the first part of the hill. Although all of the houses in Rosegarden were well maintained and none looked messy or had uncared for gardens, Ron's still stood out as being perfectly showcased. Everything was immaculate. Nothing had even the slightest glimpse of rust or mould or mildew. The weeds were scared to show themselves in Ron's garden. Tony wondered if he should wipe his shoes before walking up the path until Ron appeared at the door and beckoned him to come in.

"Thanks, Ron. I won't keep you long."

"That's alright. I've plenty of time."

Ron seemed much more genial in his home compared to how he was at the meetings.

"Cup of tea?"

"Oh no, thank you. Just a glass of water please."

Ron gestured for Tony to sit on the sofa. The room was sparsely furnished but the pieces were tasteful and of a good quality. On the wall was a Ross Roberts Rosegarden Landscape and a portrait of Ron's parents. A small television hid in the corner waiting to be switched on. In pride of place was an old radiogram with a selection of records filed away in shelves on either side. Tony went over and pulled out a few to look at. All ballet and romantic piano.

"Ah, you found my guilty pleasure. They're very lovely and great to read to."

"It's nice to find another vinyl lover. The next time I go on the hunt for some, you can come too, although I buy most of mine on line now."

"Thank you."

Tony sipped at the water. "I'm sure you know why I asked to see you, Ron."

"To see if I had any information about Frankie?"

"Yes, and also to ask about an argument you had with him on Sunday."

"Oh, of course. Well I can combine the two. We argued because he was trying to borrow money from everyone. I confronted him about it and he said he owed Charlie money. I pointed out that if borrowed to pay back Charlie, he would never be out of debt. I told him he would have to tell Charlie to wait. I was getting angry, as I sometimes do, but not at Frankie. I was enraged by that idiot Charlie. Frankie was totally gullible and Charlie treated him abysmally. I didn't know Frankie well enough to say he wasn't blameless but I do know Charlie and I hold him responsible for a lot of Frankie's less savoury behaviour."

"Thank you Ron. It seems we never got to know Frankie as we should have."

"You're right, of course. However, did the person who killed Frankie know him well?"

"If they did, they may not have killed him."

Chapter 26

The Captain was getting tired and so was Daisy. He had been in nearly every shop that catered for both locals and tourists and got the same from everyone. Frankie wasn't welcome because of his offensive behaviour. Some did say that he was just putting it on but, nevertheless, he was offensive. Nobody seemed to be that angry with him; just repelled by him. Nobody knew much about him. They said he now and then visited their shops but just to pass time and small talk and never bought anything. Tony was going to talk to the restaurateurs. Guy should've questioned his staff at the hotel. If not then, perhaps, Tony should ask that he does.

Speaking of the hotel, may as well take a little breather in the lobby.

When you entered the gold trim revolving door, the Art Deco splendour of the hotel immediately took you back to the 1930's. Comfortable scalloped shell shaped armchairs were arranged around tables with black, grey and white geometric patterns formed in the marble tops. Dotted around the side tables, long elegant women walked long elegant dogs, all with haughty, aloof looks on their long elegant faces. On the mantle of the fireplace, which took it's looks from the Chrysler building in New York, stood an angular clock that chimed every quarter of an hour despite the passage of time not effecting the rest of the room. Portraits, landscapes and abstracts in the style of Georgia O'Keefe and Tamara de Lempicka hung on the walls.

Even the drinks menu which the Captain perused, more out of a desire to be noticed by a member of the staff than to actually get any information, could have been designed, with the rest of the village, in 1923. Everything was genuine so nothing looked cheap.

"Hello, Captain. Are you and Daisy staying for lunch?"

"No, no. We're just going to have a little drink please. A bowl of water for Daisy and a Dom Papa Rum for me please. Just a single though. I haven't eaten yet. Thank you, Chloe."

"You're welcome." Chloe looked at Daisy and smiled. "You are too, Daisy."

The Captain laughed.

When Chloe came back with the rum and the water the Captain paid her and gave her a tip. "Thank you again Chloe. Before you go, what do you know about Frankie Flake?"

"He often sits in the window here. On his own. Never wants a drink or food. Just wants to sit and look out the window. When he first came here people tried talking to him but gave up. I saw him around the beach a few times, with Charlie Osborne. They just stand around and look at the women. You know, women in bikinis and swimsuits and shorts. Ogling. I feel sorry for Frankie. He seems to do it out of a sort of duty to Charlie. Like the schoolboy wanting to be thought of as cool by his mates. I saw them arguing recently. On Saturday morning as I walked to work. It was very heated. Charlie kept pointing his finger at Frankie. I couldn't hear the words though.

"Afterwards he came and sat down in the window as per usual. Just after ten when I start. I once asked him what he looked at. He said 'the infinity of the sea.' When you think about how he always behaved, it was odd for him to talk that way. Then he said about floating on the sea until he reached land. Funny, right?"

"Yes, very." Said the Captain. He wondered if anybody knew Frankie at all and why, if it was all made up, why he put on this other persona.

He sipped his Dom Papa and looked at the clock as it chimed one forty five.

"Come on, Daisy old girl. Time to meet Tony."

Chapter 27

"Well, what do you think?"

"I think we're no closer to solving this."

"I agree." Said the Captain as they walked to the Gutty Shark.

"Just a bag of chips, Captain?"

"A small sausage for Daisy too please, Tony."

Daisy upped her pace powered by a wagging tail.

"We still don't have a murder weapon do we?"

"No. It's something long and thin and cylindrical. It would have to be fairly strong as well to go in to the body and not snap."

"Are you sure it didn't snap and get lost inside?"

"Pretty sure. I had a poke around after I cleaned him."

"So something like a meat skewer or barbecue skewer made of metal."

Tony thought of the barbecue sets at Charlie Osborne's shop. "Well the ones you get in those little beach sets are a bit small. They would have to be the proper ones you get from the hardware store."

"That's the only shop I haven't checked yet. I was going there after this."

"OK. Possibly look for thick knitting needles as well."

"Knitting needles?"

"Yes. Thick, strong ones."

"OK."

Scott was waiting by the chippy's etched window which was decorated with a seascape. Central to the scene was The Cutty Sark. It always made the tourists smile or laugh when they first saw it.

Scott, Tony and the Captain stepped in to the warm and aromatic air and all immediately felt hungry.

"Good afternoon gents." Bellowed Ollie James while shaking excess oil from the chips before shovelling them out to the hot box under the display of sausages, savelroys, fritters, pies and fish.

"Are you all ready for the best chips on the south coast? Small portion with salt and vinegar, Tony? Small portion with small cod and salt no vinegar, Scott? Small portion and small plain sausage for you and Daisy, Captain?"

"What a memory you have Ollie. Salt and vinegar on my chips but not Daisy's sausage."

They watched the man work the chips and scoop out a portion.

"What can you tell us about Frankie Flake?" Tony asked.

"Frankie? I hear he went missing or legged it after he busted up one of your vans."

That bit of misinformation worked and was getting around.

"Yeah something like that. Did he ever come in here?"

"Oh yeah, all the time. The only place he ate, he told me. Means he only ate once a day then. Every day after his shift. I don't know what he did on Sundays either. Large chips with a battered jumbo sausage and no vinegar. Same order. I knew it off by heart, like most regulars' orders around here. He still told me every time. He always said the same thing about the beach too. Every time I asked him how his day was he'd say, 'not bad, not many top girls though.' One time he said it, Ross was here hanging a painting for me. One of his beautiful seascapes. That one there, actually" he said pointing to a dramatic sunset over a beach with crashing waves

"Anyway, Frankie says his 'not many top girls' thing and Ross went apeshit. First time I saw him angry."

"Really? What was said between them?"

"Ross said that Frankie and Charlie brought down the tone and that he hoped you, Tony, would fire him and that Charlie should lose his shop. At the very least he wanted him not to come back this year. But back he came. I'm not sure if Ross saw him this year or not."

"I'm beginning to think he did." Said Tony. "So, did he say anything else besides the pervy remark?"

129

"We'll that's the funny thing. He never said it in a pervy way. Just matter of fact. Like ordering his chips or talking about the weather. Just something to say. I know it's not in keeping with the village but he could have said it about anything. It's like he's trying to put on a front and doesn't know how to stop."

"That's not the first time I've heard that today." The Captain said looking round at the others.

"I had one of the tradeswomen say that to me. Or similar."

"Hm. Why did he act like that?"

"Well if he turns up again we'll find out. Now, gents, wooden forks to go with the food. How about drinks? Cokes all round?"

They walked out and headed to a bench to watch the sea while eating their deep fried delights. Daisy wolfed down her chopped up sausage and stared at the three men eating.

"Well, plenty of people disliked him. Some had heated arguments with him. A few saw a different side of him. One person killed him. We know those in the first three categories and we're bound to find more. But what about the one in the fourth. Who the hell are they?"

Scott and the Captain nodded in agreement and the seagulls that flew overhead, waiting for fallen scraps, laughed at them and mocked them, for only the seagulls saw it happen.

Chapter 28

Scott drove the ancient blue and white, Police issue , Morris Minor out the village and took a left two miles down the road, up the hill, away from the sea and into the countryside.

"Have you ever thought of asking for a newer car, Scott?"

"I've avoided it so far because I don't want to be on the radar. Now I've phoned in to ask for info about the mystery dark green car I'll need to wait another couple of years to stay off the radar."

Tony laughed.

"I suppose nobody high up ever bothers you down here. Does it ever worry you that there isn't enough crime to warrant an onsite police presence?"

"No. Apparently, the chief of the county police and Guy Lambert have an agreement whereby the funding from the police and Rosegarden is fifty-fifty. Guy likes the idea of a Bobby on display for the tourists. As you're about to see, the farmers want me here as well."

They had driven to the farthest farm. The journey from the road to the farm house was lined by fruit orchards. Apples, pears, plums and cherries all grew on the farm and were in bloom. Both men smiled at the sight. Beyond the farmhouse, in the distance, the farmers and seasonal staff were busy sowing vegetables. They parked by the farmhouse and were greeted by a goat and a barking dog. The goat looked at the dog with amused nonchalance and then slowly strutted away looking for something to eat. The dog kept barking.

"Keep your bloody noise down, Prince. What's wrong? Who's there?"

"Afternoon, Ruth."

"Nice to see you, Ruth"

"Oh hello, you two."

Ruth smiled at them and wiped her hands dry on an old towel. "Come on in, I'll put the kettle on."

Prince trotted off to see what the goat was up to.

It was the first time Tony had been inside this farmhouse. "Wow. This is very impressive, Ruth. It's like the after shots in a makeover programme."

"Thank you. We love it, too." Ruth gathered cups and teabags and put the kettle on without asking. "Did you want to speak to Joe? He's not long gone out to supervise the sowing."

"No that's fine. You two are always together and always talk so you probably know the same things anyway."

"What things, Scott"

"Well Frankie Flake has gone missing and we were wondering if you have seen him at all. You know, running across the fields or anything out of the ordinary. Have you seen anyone drive past or further up the road you don't recognise?"

"Frankie Flake the ice cream man? Missing? Oh dear. He sometimes worked for us in the early autumn after his stint selling ice cream. Such a lovely man. Always polite. Very quiet but never rude."

"Really? He worked for you and was nice?"

"Oh I know what the people of the village think, Tony. But up here he is different from what they say. Even when we go down there and see him he is polite."

"So do you recall any strange occurrences recently?"

"No. I saw Frankie when he came back. On his way into Rosegarden. He walked from the bus stop by the Crows Nest. He said he came back out of duty for his late uncle but it would be his last year. He didn't enjoy it and said he was bored and fed up pretending to be someone he wasn't."

"Did he say anymore about what he meant by that?"

"I think he acted a certain way for that Charlie."

"OK. What else?"

"Well, not much else to tell really." Ruth put her hand on her chin and thought a moment. "Actually, I tell a lie. Last week that Charlie Osborne came up here when Frankie was visiting. I think

he was looking for him and Frankie says to me 'please don't let him know I'm here. I want to enjoy this person for a little longer."
"This person?" Scott asked "What did he mean?"
"I have no idea. Maybe he meant the nice Frankie on the farm and not the one selling ice cream. I don't know though."
"OK. Well thanks Ruth."
"If you find Frankie, let him know he's welcome up here on our farm."
"We will, Ruth. We will."

*

For the first ten minutes of the journey they drove along in silence.
"I'm starting to think we've missed something. I don't know if we would get closer to finding out who the killer is if we hadn't missed something though."
"I agree, Scott. It's strange how he put on different faces for different people."
"It's my guess that he gravitated to the one person he knew, Charlie, and then acted the way he thought he should. It must be hard to change appearances and say 'No. This is really me. Not that person you're used to seeing'."
"I guess. Doesn't bring us any closer to the killer though."
"No but it's interesting. Makes you think about how much truth you see around you."
"Jeez, Scott. That's as deep as a fat man's navel."
For the last mile of the journey they slipped back to silence and their own thoughts.
"Here we are. Kittyhawk Farm. Old man Hawkins knows and trusts me, Tony, so let me do the talking."
"I have met him before, Scott. I admit I was twelve and he chased me across his field because he caught me and his youngest daughter exploring the differences between male and female."
Scott laughed. How old was she?"
"Sixteen. She already knew the differences and I had a good idea."

"We'll I'm sure after thirty plus years he'll have forgotten all about it."

"Are you sure you know him?"

They pulled up and Scott honked his horn. A few faces appeared at windows on all sides of the courtyard. Hawkins appeared at the doorway. His face contorted and from it came the words "Sergeant Hayward." He looked at Tony. "Martini. I remember you. Marlene isn't here. Nor is Nellie or Lizzie."

Tony laughed. "I told you he'd remember me."

"Yes but you only mentioned one daughter."

"Well, what do you want?"

"Tony and I are asking everyone what they can tell us about Frankie Flake, or if they noticed anything strange lately, especially on Sunday night. He's disappeared."

"Well, can't say as I blame him. Only met him twice. Seemed alright though easily led by Charlie Osborne. Osborne is not welcome here. Caught him in my field once. Long lens on his camera pointed at my house." He looked at Tony. "At least you were man enough to mess around with them. Osborne needed a tripod, coz he was busy with one hand. So busy he didn't here me come up behind him. Pervert. My grand daughter Chrissy talked with Frankie a few times. I'll get her."

"Funny how two of his daughters and their husbands decided to stay with the miserable old bugger to work on his farm."

"Again, the side we see may be the opposite of the side they see."

"You've become quite the philosopher since this happened."

"Well it does make you think"

Chrissy came to the door and smiled. "'ey you two. What's this about Frankie disappearing? I like buying my ice cream there. Only yesterday I got a double scoop. Better than that soft stuff."

"That's a shame. He has gone off and the van was damaged too. No more scoops of ice cream for you I'm afraid." Tony smiled "So you were a regular of Frankie's?"

"Yeah. I often go on a Sunday and sometimes after dinner, in the summer evenings, during the week to walk on the beach or 'ave a dip in the sea. It's good to get away now and then. I like to feel the sea breeze on my face and stretch out my arms and worship the sun. Frankie laughs and says I'm a real hoot."

"Did you say you saw him on Sunday? What time would that have been?" Scott got out his notebook. He had hardly used it before Frankie's death but since had almost filled it.

"Oh around three I'd say. 'e seemed a little distracted, maybe thoughtful. 'e said 'e didn't like Rosegarden anymore. Especially since 'e fell out with Charlie. I told 'im that the other people of the village were alright. 'e said it was too late. People wouldn't talk to 'im. You know it's that Charlie's fault. 'e 'as such a grip on him."

"We know they're friends. What do you mean by a grip?"

"Well, Tony, Charlie always tells 'im what to do and almost 'ow to think and who is good and bad in the village. 'e even got Frankie to take pictures of the women for 'im."

"Did he tell you that?"

"Yeah, but I believe 'im. 'e was so embarrassed when I caught 'im taking one of me. I was there in my bikini, arms outstretched to the sun. I turned around and there 'e was with this camera. 'e went bright red and apologised. Apparently Charlie asked 'im to do it because 'e was stuck in his shop all day. Bloody lie. I've seen 'im up 'ere in the week in working 'ours. On 'is way to Molly I bet."

Scott scribbled away and Tony asked. "Are you sure about that?"

"Yeah. Charlie 'ad all the passcodes to 'Frankie's iPhone and iPad. 'e forgot it once and Charlie came to the van all angry and unlocked it for 'im. Frankie was embarrassed and Charlie called 'im a dumb Wop. I don't think 'e did forget. I reckons Charlie changed them without telling 'im."

"When was that?"

"Beginning of the season last year. Then you banned 'im from keeping 'is phone when 'e worked in the middle of last season."

"Yes I did."

"Poor Frankie, 'e's gone to parts unknown. All alone in this world."
"Yes, poor Frankie. Well thanks, Chrissy. You've been helpful and we appreciate it."

*

"Well, that was a turn up, eh, Tony?"
"Yes it was. Made me realise what we overlooked and I'm pretty stupid for not thinking of it. His camera and his notebook in the van. What can they tell us. Also, what times were his iPhone and iPad used? If it was during his working hours we know that it was probably Charlie who used them."
"Yes. Never thought of that."
"Come on, let's meet with Molly. This should be interesting. If he was pervy she would pick up on it."
They drove as if heading back to the village on the last quarter of the semi-circular road and then went down a narrow lane with wheat fields either side. After a short while the lane widened a little and the wheat gave way to canola at the end of which was a well looked after farm yard, in complete contrast to the Kittyhawk farm. In the distance, beyond the farmhouse, were lavender fields.
"There she is now."
Molly was walking towards them with an axe in one hand and a log basket in the other.
Tony put his hands up. "Jesus Christ, Molly. We're only here for a chat!"
Molly gave out a loud laugh. "Well, well. Two handsome gents have come calling. Or did you want to speak to my husband?"
"You, really. I mean if he's around we'd speak to Laurie as well."
"He's working hard in the fields at the moment, Scott. What can I do for you?"
Tony couldn't figure out whether everything Molly said was sexual or whether her appearance in jean shorts and a blouse unbuttoned enough to reveal cleavage, along with an ever present naughty smile and twinkle in her eye played tricks on him.

"Well, Frankie Flake has disappeared and we were wondering what you could tell us about him or if you saw anything strange this last weekend."

"Oh, Frankie. What a sweetie. I mean he would struggle to make eye contact with me but he always seemed so shy and polite."

"Really?"

"Oh I know what the people of the village thought, but then, I know what they think of me. Flirty, dirty, slutty, shows off too much flesh and all those things. I'm proud of the way I look and I like to show it off. I like to flirt a little too. The only man I let close to what I show off is my husband. People think Fisher comes up here and plays around. That's laughable. He plays around with Laurie. Sometimes has a game of chess with him, but that's all. Those two are good mates and he looks out for me. That's all. People see what they want to see. That includes Frankie too. Poor bugger was ostracised early on and looked to that perv Charlie. Now he, is a filthy bastard. According to Frankie he showed him nudes of me. Bloody cheek. My husband took those. We were fooling around. When we were gone one weekend somebody broke in. Stole some knickers and those photos. Now I know who. There you go Scott, arrest him for theft."

"I'll certainly question him again." They didn't mention what Charlie had said about her.

"Was there an altercation between Bill Fisher and Frankie outside the Fisherman's?"

Molly thought about it with a confused expression. "Oh, bloody hell. Last year? It wasn't a fight or even an argument. A misunderstanding, that's all. Frankie obviously believed what Charlie told him about me and Fisher. He asked if he could double date. You know, me and Fisher and him and my sister. I laughed but Fisher got heated. I calmed him down and told Frankie to apologise to everyone. He did and walked away crestfallen."

There was a pause while everyone took it in.

"I get what you're saying, Molly. We certainly need to stop thinking about Frankie the way we do."

"Yeah, Tony, you do."

Tony looked in to her eyes and saw more imploring than the anger all her words came out with.

"How about the weekend. Anything weird happen?" Scott broke the silence.

"No. Nothing that I can think of. Now, if that's all, I need to chop some firewood."

"Thanks, Molly. It's good to see things in a different way."

"Yes, thank you."

"Stick around. When I get warmed up I'll be swinging the axe in my underwear"

Tony laughed. Scott blushed.

"Oh, Scott, by the way, you should let people see your other side too. You do live in Rosegarden after all."

Scott blushed more.

Chapter 29

Rosegarden Hardware had everything you could ever want for basic DIY and more. It was the largest store and, with the need for symmetry and pattern, it was in the middle of the run of stores aimed at the locals, but open to everyone.

At the end of the household paint aisle, or as the Captain called it, the Rainbow Aisle, was the crafts section. He went straight to it and found what he was looking for.

"No Daisy, today, Captain?"

"Oh hello Jocelyn. Well, she had quite the morning, walking all over Rosegarden and on the beach. Poor things fast asleep in her bed."

"Ah. She is a little cutie. So is there something I can help you with?"

"Well, firstly, do you have any barbecue equipment?"

"Sorry, Captain. We stopped selling barbecue equipment when the ban came in. That was a few years ago now. We don't even stock the skewers, forks or tongs."

"Oh, of course. How silly of me. I was hoping to have one in the back garden but no matter."

"Some people buy them online. You could try that."

"Yes, I could try that. Maybe Danny could help me. Anyway, I was browsing the craft section because I will need some oils and a pallet knife. I'm not as good as Ross but I like to do it for the fun. Anyway I noticed these knitting needles. I have no idea who would use them or what they're for. They're huge."

"Ah yes, those ten millimetre ones. People use them to knit things like thick cable stitch and things like that."

"Oh I see. Is there much call for that?"

"In Rosegarden? Of course! All the touristy fishermen's sweaters are knitted here and so are some of the other souvenirs."

"Oh. I thought they were bought in. Pardon my ignorance."

"No, no, no. A group of us make them. We have a knitting circle that meets every Tuesday and Thursday evening."

The Captain often wondered who came up with the notion of older and wiser as, in his experience, the older you get the more people expect you to be ignorant and accept it if you are. Jocelyn was quite content to answer his stupid questions, and a little patronising, but that was alright, his questions were stupid. The answers would lead on to other less stupid and more probing questions and Jocelyn would still think he was old and daft.

"A whole circle of people, eh? Let me guess some of the members."

The Captain paused for dramatic effect. "Maggie is probably in charge. There will also be you, of course, possibly Mama Cassandra, Kam Dhaji. Hm. Can't think who else."

"Well you've made the mistake of thinking it's all women. Maggie is the leader, sort of. The Ling brothers and their wives, Kim and Sue, come as do the Fab Four. Mama Cassandra no. Kam Dhaji yes. And, of course Sergeant Scott Hayward."

"Well goes to show how little I know. Maybe I could join. "

"If you like. All are welcome"

"Do you have many of those big needles? Do they come in different materials or colours?"

"Funny you should ask, we do actually. Some with colourful swirly patterns. They're plastic. Most are wood. But we also had a stainless steel pair until recently."

"Really? Much call for those?"

"No. We sold it last week, after forever."

"Not a quick seller. Must have been an experienced knitter to buy those."

"Yes. Scott broke his wooden ones and decided steel would be a better bet. He's very good."

"Is he really? He's never mentioned that."

"Yes. He often teaches the newer members. He was quite upset on Saturday when he bought them. I think his old wooden ones were very old."

Chapter 30

Date night. Tony was as excited and nervous as a boy at the year six disco. It was daft really. He'd known Emma May for most of his life but with his moving to London and her getting married not long after, and then both of them running businesses, it meant they just smiled in passing and greeted each other now and then and that was all. When they spoke yesterday, it was the longest conversation they'd had since they were teenagers.

He put on his most expensive cologne and best Hawaiian shirt. A mint condition, original, 1950s, Alfred Shaheen Surf N Sand shirt in golds and browns and black on a white background, depicting stylised fish and shells.

It was going to be a welcome distraction from finding Frankie Flake's killer. Quite a few people had motives to dislike him but none strong enough to kill him. There was no murder weapon, but several suggestions. It was vague and so were the perceptions of Frankie. Nobody really knew him that well. All the farmers liked him and saw a different Frankie to the one that everyone in the village seemed to see. This was definitely Charlie's influence.

With the official line being that he disappeared it was difficult to ask anyone for their movements at a certain time without causing suspicion.

What did the two from London have to do with it, if anything? He'd find out tomorrow, perhaps. Scott had got the address from records. The car was licensed to a company called Executive Services in London. Possibly false plates. Possibly a cover operation. He had no idea. But Frankie did have a business card with that name on in his effects"

"Penny for your thoughts, Mr Martini."

Tony looked up and saw Emma May who had made as much of an effort as he had.

"Wow. You look absolutely amazing." he said standing up.

"Thank you."

"Hang on. Is that dress vintage Shaheen?"

"Yep. Surf N Sand. I'd get a boiler suit made from Shaheen if I could but it would break my heart if it got dirty."

They both laughed and Tony thought he was in heaven.

They got behind the table in the booth and smiled at each other.

"I'm starving. What's your special tonight?"

"For the meat eaters it's Spaghetti Chorizo Carbonara. For the veggies it's Lentil Linguine Ragu."

"I'm veggie so the linguine for me."

"Red wine? Cocktail? Beer?"

"Do you do a French Martini?"

"Paul is a great bartender and an expert at cocktails."

Tony ordered garlic bread, the same mains and a Moretti for himself as well as Emma May's cocktail.

"So you collect Shaheen too? How did I not know this? How is it I know very little about you? Let me take inventory. I'll tell you what I know."

Emma May smiled and winked. "I can't wait to hear all about myself."

"OK. You were three years below me at school. You're a Rosegardener by heritage, like me. You married an outsider called Will who took over your dad's garage when he died. You guys divorced after four years and one son, the one and only Glenn May. You're a great mechanic and a better businesswoman. I now know that you collect Shaheen. Oh and you also have the prettiest blue eyes I've ever seen."

He couldn't believe he said it. But there it was, out there. Emma May smiled and blushed a little although it wasn't noticed in the low light.

"Thank you Mr Martini."

The garlic bread and drinks arrived.

"To Alfred Shaheen!" Tony toasted and they clinked glasses.

"Wow. That's a delicious French Martini and pretty strong too."

"Too strong? I'll get it changed."

"No, just stronger than restaurants and pubs usually make them. It's delicious." Emma took another sip and smiled and licked her lips.

"OK. So you know basic historical facts about me but you don't know anything about me. I love being a mechanic. Have done ever since I was a little girl helping my dad. I knew I'd take the business over one day. My childhood crush, the one I wanted to marry, moved to London when I was twenty and he was twenty three."

Tony nearly choked on his beer.

"So I married a man I had met at a car show. We were both mechanics and he loved the idea of having a garage in a seaside village. I liked him a lot but thought I loved him. So we got married and before I could say carburettor he had taken over the business completely. Dad died a month afterwards. I thought having a baby would be a good excuse not to be around the garage. By the time Glenn started school, Will had made a mess of the business and started going away to be with another woman. We divorced when Glenn was seven. He agreed to let me take back the garage. I built it up and made a success of it. This dress was bought to celebrate my first year of making a five grand profit. It was the start of me collecting Shaheen. I wear Shaheen when I go away for weekends, which isn't often. Glenn is a bit of a one at the moment but I love my son and I know he'll be a good man one day. When I'm not working I love hot baths, long walks, painting, watching movies, I've posed for Ross a few times, fully clothed of course, and I enjoy a takeaway from Sanjiv Gupta's curry house once in a while. Why don't Italian restaurants ever offer takeaways? Anyway. Now you know more about me."

Tony sipped some beer as the mains were served.

"This week I have realised that I walk around with my eyes closed and have done for years. How could I not have noticed you more and known more about you? Your schoolgirl crush?"

"I tried dropping hints now and then but you never noticed. Molly and I used to think you were gay or just totally engrossed in your own little world."

"Molly is a character. I spoke to her today. Straight forward, says it how it is and very proud of what she has."

"You can say that again." Emma laughed. "I would be as well if I looked like her."

"You look just as good, believe me."

"Mr Martini, you'll make me blush."

"Tony to you."

"I've known Molly since we were little girls at school and I know how she is. What did she tell you that makes you think that way?"

"Well, everyone complained about Frankie Flake when I asked about him. I never knew there was a problem. They said Charlie Osborne was a fellow pervert of his. I never knew. But then again nor did Guy Lambert. I think he's avoided Caught In A Dream. Anyway, when Scott and I visited the farms today, everyone said the opposite about Frankie. Molly more or less told me that I don't see things or notice how Frankie really was."

"You're a busy man, Tony. Restaurant, two ice cream vans and called on to help out Scott all the time. So come on. Forget that and tell me about you. Oh. This food is delicious by the way."

"I'm glad you're enjoying it."

Emma May gave him time to get his history straight in his head.

"Well as you know, I inherited this restaurant from my dad. I never wanted it when I was young. I wanted excitement. I wanted to be of Italian descent and in the mob. Not serving lasagne to tourists. Rosegarden was nice but I needed more. Or I thought I did. So I went to London looking for something, I didn't know what, but something. I wasn't there long when I got in a fight with two doormen and walked away unharmed. I'm not bragging just telling what happened. Anyway, the owner of the club hired me as his heavy, come bodyguard, come fixer. I did some horrible things for some horrible people. I made lots of money and earned respect. Just thought I was the dog's bollocks. Then it all went downhill."

He took a drink of beer and looked at Emma May as if he wasn't sure if he should go on.

"Go on. I'm prepared for the worst."

"No you're not." He looked around the room to see if anyone could hear or was listening. A few looked over and waved.

"What's past has passed. Tell me everything. Warts and all."

Another mouthful of food and a sip or two of beer and he carried on.

"The boss acted as judge and jury and I carried out the punishment. Whatever he said. He had me over a barrel because of all the things I had done previously and he always only gave the harshest sentence to gang members or bent coppers or the John's who had severely mistreated the girls. Yes there was that side to the business too.

"After a while it became relentless. There was a screw loose in the boss's head and I acted out what he couldn't do. It went from weekly to daily and I just became numb to everything. I made up my mind to leave the life after I had to witness a female fixer punish one of the girls. Mimi, the female fixer, loved inflicting pain on the poor woman. I wanted to intervene and give her a taste of it but I couldn't."

He looked at Emma May who looked absorbed and shocked by the story.

"What did she do?"

"She tried to escape the life. She wanted to escape from the John's and the boss and people like me and Mimi. She actually, naively, wrote a resignation letter and gave two weeks notice. Mimi thought that was hilarious. So did the boss. We went over to hear her out. When it was clear that she just wanted to quit and not go through some other pimp I thought they'd let her off and let her go. Instead Mimi scarred her face and broke her fingers one by one. This was in the back of the boss's car. They told me to drive them to Oxford Street. When we got there they threw her naked in to the street. I made the car disappear in to traffic before anybody noticed us.

"The next day the police got an anonymous tip off and we were arrested and all the offices and computers searched.

"The boss got life in prison with a minimum of thirty years, Mimi and I got eight years each."

"Why. Not being judgemental, Tony, but if you," she looked around and leant in and whispered "hurt so many people, you should have got much longer."

"Agreed. But, firstly only one person I hospitalised wasn't part of organised crime and they didn't care about the rest and, secondly, I was the one who tipped them off. I told them everything they needed to put the boss away. They'd been after him for a long time. They looked the other way when it came to the disappearances of gang members."

They sat in silence for a moment while the dishes were taken away.

"Dessert?"

She silently shook her head then said "I'll have another drink though."

The waiter came back with another beer and another French Martini.

"Who knew you were in prison? Nobody mentioned it here?"

"Guy Lambert visited me and I spoke to my dad on the phone. Both made me realise what a mess I'd made of life. As soon as my sentence was over I came back. My dad hardly spoke to me to start with. Then he saw how hard I was trying to fit in and make something of myself and the restaurant.

"You were there at his seventieth birthday, right?"

"Yes. It was a great night. The whole village celebrated with him."

"Exactly. That was the night he told me he forgave me and was proud of me at last. He retired the next day and died ten years after."

"I remember the service and his funeral."

"Well that was my story. I don't like it but at least the last third has been good. Back home at Rosegarden with my restaurant and good people."

Emma May studied him. "You're scary."

"I shouldn't have told you."

"Yes you should. I like honesty even if it is unpleasant."

"Very unpleasant."

"OK that was your history but what about you? Why Shaheen? What other interests? Why are you single?"

"I loved the shirt on Elvis's album Blue Hawaii and tracked one down and became interested in Alfred Shaheen and his designs. I love scuba diving and coastal walks and listening to the sea and running this restaurant and my Connie's ice cream van. I'm single because I know I couldn't have shared my story with anyone. I shared it with you because I like you a lot."

"I like you too, Tony. But I want you to know that I'm used to my independence and I don't want any serious relationship that disrupts that. I'm sure you don't either. You do frighten me a little. Or, should I say, your past frightens me a lot. That said if you want to stay at mine tonight I can take you up to London in my Mustang tomorrow."

Tony laughed. "Sounds good to me. All of it."

Chapter 31

From her bedroom window there was a clear view of the sea and the clear blue sky and seagulls that danced to their own screeching songs and they woke with the sun in their eyes and smiled at each other and kissed and made love again and then lay and talked softly about nothing and with the pauses between sentences they could hear the village waking up and in the quietest moments they could hear the sea whispering to the shore and in those moments they looked deeply in to each others eyes and smiled at the soul that they had found in each other and realised that these were the other halves of their souls that had been missing.

Then the moment broke. From downstairs came the sounds of Glenn moving around.

"I can't wait to see the expression on Glenn's face when he sees me."

Emma May punched his shoulder gently. "Don't be mean about my little boy."

"He's six foot two and looks like you feed him on hay, how is that little?"

Glenn almost choked on his cereal when Tony appeared in the kitchen.

"Morning, Glenn"

"Er. Morning. Mr Martini." He said with quick glances that bounced from his mother to her lover.

"Can you look after the garage today, love? I'm driving Tony to London and then picking him up later. You can close up at two if you want."

"OK." He chewed and refilled his mouth in slow motion and eyed Tony cautiously.

"I'll be back in a mo. Just going to shower and change and see my staff before we go. I'll meet you here."

*

A couple of hours later they were roaring through the countryside heading towards the motorway singing along with the songs they knew on the radio and talking through the ones they didn't. They could have been heading to a favourite picnic spot or a weekend in a holiday cottage but the closer they got to the motorway, the more cars and vans and trucks and coaches and motorbikes multiplied exponentially and so did the realities that faced Tony. He smiled and pretended that nothing was going to happen.

"So what are you going to be shopping for when I'm snooping around London?"

"Whatever I see that speaks to me. Could be shoes, bags, books, tools. Anything. I know a few good vintage emporiums and charity shops.

"What are you going to be snooping for?"

"Whatever I see that speaks to me. Honestly, I have no idea what I'll find. I don't know the area or the company that the car is registered to. It might be a total flop or it could give me information about Frankie's killer."

In their moments together he had told her about Frankie being found dead.

"Please be careful. I know you used to do this sort of thing regularly and could look after yourself but that was years ago. I don't want to say goodbye so soon after we've got together."

"I promise I'll be careful and only pick fights if I need to. I'm not putting myself in danger for the likes of Frankie Flake, no matter how curious I am."

They were nearing London when he told her to drop him off and pick him up at Barnes Station. Emma dropped him off and went to Richmond to shop.

Chapter 32

London is always changing. Small landmarks like pubs, cafes and shops often close or change hands and are unrecognisable after a refurbishment and go from The Nags Head to The Noble Horse or from The Hasty Tasty to the Happy Vegan.

Even the demographic changes in some areas as working class neighbourhoods become sought after by more affluent people and in other areas immigrants from one culture give way to immigrants from another and the melting pot of the country gets stirred and mixed to a richer flavour.

The only things that don't change are the major landmarks and the Tube. Tony knew the system like he knew the streets of Rosegarden. After getting in to Central London from Barnes he navigated his way to the station nearest to the address Scott gave him.

He didn't know the area that well so he took direction from his iPhone and arrived in a well to do neighbourhood that seemed to be a mix of coffee bars, offices and high rent apartments. In the middle of the second block he saw what looked like a solid door with opaque glass panels. Etched in the top pane were the words EXECUTIVE SERVICES. There was no parking anywhere on the street. Some of the apartments had openings that led to underground car parks. He looked at the door again and wondered what approach he needed. Then he noticed it. No doorbell, no intercom and no post box anywhere.

A postman came walking along, sorting out the next letterbox full of post.

"Morning postie, I need to speak to a bloke who works here. Any idea how to get in?" Without realising or trying, Tony's London accent went up at least three levels. The rural South coast was a long way away.

"Well he could've told ya to go in the back." The postie looked up quickly then looked at his post again. "When I first did this round I couldn't figure it. Not that they get any post that is. Must be all digital or something. But I did the parcels one day and my mate Badger told me that the parcels are round the back. Bit weird though. Nobody answered the bell but a voice from the inside says leave the parcel on the doorstep. I told Badger about it and he says I was lucky I didn't have to deal with Arnie. That's what Badger calls him. Muscles on muscles. Arms like string bags full of walnuts. Anyway good luck. Your mate ain't Arnie is he?"

"No definitely not. Thanks for the tip."

"No probs. Best be getting a move on.'

Tony watched the postie walk away quickly, then looked around before going around the side of the building. It led to an alleyway filled with wheelie bins, vans unloading in to Goods-In entrances and cars parked tightly together. There, halfway down, was the dark green car.

He wondered how he would get inside. Knocking on the door wouldn't cut it.

Walking over to the car he noticed he was being watched by a huge muscular figure in the doorway and a CCTV camera pointing at the area around the door. Tony gave the car the once over and looked inside. Handgrips were placed neatly in the well between the front seats. There was nothing else in the car. He slowly walked around the car. Stopping at the driver's side he stooped down and put his nose against the glass leaving a greasy smear.

"Lost something? Why the fuck are you looking in my car?"

The giant muscleman, immaculately dressed, was staring down at him.

"Just admiring it. My friend had one of these. Not as clean as yours though. Do the hand grip exercisers come as standard?"

"Being funny? You some sort of smart arse?"

"No. But I have to apologise for leaving fingerprints on the paintwork. I think I got a grease smudge from my nose on your window too."

"What the fuck? Where?"

Tony wiped the outside of his nose with his finger and smeared it on the door and then spat on the window.

"Right there."

"Fuck you." Muscles bounded down the stairs and threw a wild punch. Tony read it before the muscle packed shoulder turned and dodged it and got inside and grabbed him by the genitals and squeezed with all his strength. Muscles screamed and bent double and Tony brought his knee up and made contact with Muscle's nose which flowered red all over his face. Tony gave some quick punches to Muscles bloody face and the big man collapsed against his clean car smearing a blood red mark down the side.

From behind Tony came a whistle and a slow clap.

"You made a mess of him." Tony guessed it was the other man from the green car and turned around to see a gun pointed at him.

"The boss was watching on CCTV. Come with me."

Tony caught his breath, straightened and tidied himself and followed the directions of the gun. He hadn't done anything like that for years and it showed.

Through the bare concrete hallways of the back areas, Tony followed directions grunted at him by the man who jabbed the gun in his back. They entered a carpeted foyer and went up two flights of stairs. Everywhere smelled of expensive diffusers and the odd trace of fragrance left behind from someone unknown. It reminded Tony of upmarket hotels. The only thing missing was the smell of coffee, the occasional ting of an elevator door and people. Everywhere was quiet. It was easy to imagine that just the two of them and the unseen boss were the last people in the world.

They stopped behind a frosted glass door and the gunman knocked. "Enter." The voice was somehow familiar to Tony. They entered a giant office with glass walls that gave views down the street and the buildings opposite.

"Well, well. I thought it was you. The genital crushing squeeze followed by the knee to the nose. Classic Tony Martini."

The gunman raised his eyebrows.

"Yes, Maxi. This is Tony Martini. He's either out of practice or he wanted to come inside and see what was here. Otherwise that gun would be sticking out your arse. You're a legend, Tony. Well at least to some of the underworld and wannabe hard men like Maxi here."

The two of them stared at each other.

"It's been a long time, Tony. Don't you have anything to say to me?"

"Hello, Mimi."

Mimi half stood, half sat, with her bum on the desk. She was power suited and high heel booted and every inch the boss.

"I didn't expect to see you here."

"You didn't? Well what did you expect? Why are you here picking fights with poor defenceless musclemen?"

"It's all a bit weird and taken me by surprise. What is this operation you have here? Nobody's around except for Maxi, here, and Muscles."

"Butch."

"You're kidding me?"

"No, his name is Butch. Now, I asked my questions first. It's my territory and there's still a gun pointed at you. Talk."

"Some people asked me to find out why their ice cream man was missing, possibly bumped off by two heavies who went to their little, peaceful, seaside village, in a car that matches the description of that one in your alleyway. Francis Fenelli, aka Frankie Flake sent emails and text messages to this place, Maxi and Butch show up then Frankie goes missing presumed dead. What's going on Mimi. I want to go back to the village and give them an idea then go back to my nice retired peaceful life."

"Well, you're wrong about the emails and texts. Yes someone sent them but to a burner phone of ours not associated with this establishment. I guess you made the assumption based on the car's license plate. Anyway, I didn't order him to be killed and my boys didn't kill him. Someone said he had info for us about a member of the month. He said he recognised someone from our board and wanted payment for info. Of course we would have found the member of the month and then beaten up the informer without paying him."

"I'm lost. What is this Member of the Month thing. How did Frankie now about Executive Services? He's an ice cream man and a drifter, not an executive."

"You really are out of the loop aren't you?"

"I retired from the life when I got out of nick. I do a little PI work now and then. Nothing major. Like I said, a village up the coast from where I live asked me to find Frankie Flake. Biggest case I've had. So tell me what you know about Frankie and I'll scoot along, report what I found, aka nothing, and pick up my earnings to pay for next months groceries."

Mimi looked him up and down and studied him. There was no way of knowing what she thought about him. He hardly knew what she thought of him, or anyone, back in the day. He could only imagine that he had dropped in her esteem. From feared hard man to supposed PI trying to pay next months bills.

"You can leave us now Maxi. Go see if Butch is ok and help him if he needs it.

Once the gunman had left she continued. "OK Tony, I'll be straight with you. We have no beef and I can see you need a little help with all this. We rent out very high class girls from here. I'll show you the Member of the Month board in a moment."

She sat down behind her desk and motioned for Tony to sit. He let himself relax a little in a designer armchair that probably cost more than his restaurant.

"We have a regular we call Double Trouble. He told us a friend of his had come in to a bit of money and wanted a good time. The friend, who called himself Frank Francis, was going to pay for both Double Trouble and himself to have a Sunday with a girl each. It was OK. It went smoothly. Then, a couple of months later, Double Trouble tells me they want the same again. Well, I agreed to it. This time though Frank Francis, or Eyebrows as we called him, didn't want to do anything but talk to his girl. That would have been fine but he refused to pay the full fee. He said he just wanted to talk and why should he pay for anything else. He ran off and left enough for half the fee of his girl and nothing for Double Trouble."

"So Eyebrows pissed off everybody, both girls, Double Trouble and you."

"Correct. That said, I didn't care about the girls too much. I lined them up with other clients shortly after. We accompanied Double Trouble to the bank and got the money from him. Eyebrows became a Member of the Month."

"You went to the cashpoint with him?"

"No, better than that. He has a safety deposit box. Maxi went in the room with him while he got the cash out. He had quite a bit in there apparently."

Tony started to understand the Member of the Month idea.

Come on, let me show you the rogues gallery or Member of the Month board. Call it what you will.

Tony followed her back to the foyer. The photo board was a metre by a metre and a half and had thirteen photos on it. The thirteenth photo, in the middle of the board and larger than the rest was a photo of Detective Sergeant Cooper, the man who arrested the original gang. The others were arranged neatly with a month named below each.

"Recognise anyone, Tony?"

"Yep, Eyebrows is Frankie Flake. So that's why your boys went to rough him up?"

"Yeah. I told them to just give him the once over but not to kill him. By a lot of standards it was a minor offence. They didn't find him anyway. Maxi gave me the full report. They got pissed off waiting, Butch's OCD went in to overdrive and he cleaned and tidied everything in sight. Maxi had fun with him and tipped out his ashtray then got pissed off waiting as well and shot some ice cream van or other."

"That explains a lot. It was his ice cream van so you probably scared him enough to up and leave."

"He'll stay on the board a little longer."

Tony looked at the board again.

"Why is Detective Sergeant Cooper up there?"

"Detective Superintendent Cooper now. I like everyone to know what he looks like. Did you visit or speak to The Boss before he died?"

"No. I just wanted to fade away in to obscurity and peaceful retirement."

"Yet here you are."

"I had no idea about all this."

"I know you well Tony and I believe you."

They both studied the wall.

"So it wasn't Frankie who messaged you it was Double Trouble?"

"Yes."

"Why have they all got nicknames?"

"People we deal with seldom give us their real names so we came up with these. Either who they look like, for example Churchill there. Paid with fake notes. We only take cash for obvious reasons. It has its problems but worth it. Sir Galahad paid but never had sex. Nothing wrong with that but he talked the girl out of working for me. Gail we called her. Spelled G A I L but because she blew like a G A L E.

"George Best seemed OK but beat up one of the girls. We got there too late but she survived and went back to work two weeks later. Shaggy looked so much like the cartoon character that the girl he was with couldn't stop laughing when he told her he had a Great Dane."

"So he hit her?"

"What? No but he did go extra rough on her without paying extra."

Tony nodded but felt sick.

"And the months?"

"With each new offender the oldest one, January, will get taken off the board and all the others rotated back one. Anyway, recognise any?"

"No, but some really do look like their namesakes. Tyson is the spitting image of pre tattoo Iron Mike."

"Yes. He wanted it rougher than we allow. By the time Butch and Maxi got to the room he had scarpered. We'll find him, I'm sure. We almost always do."

"Are you still after Frankie Flake?"

"Even if he was still in that seaside village it's not worth the bother. If we come across him we may have a few words to say. We don't know where he is and we don't care."

Tony studied the board again.

"OK. So tell me, who is Double Trouble? I don't see him on the board."

"He hasn't done anything to go on there. He's repugnant and I wouldn't talk to him if it weren't for business, but he's not an offender."

"Does the name Charlie Osborne mean anything?"

"No, Tony." Mimi looked from the board to Tony and smiled.

"Are you still an Elvis fan, Tony?"

"I love his music and the fact he wore Shaheen."

"I'll give you a clue. Elvis and Double Trouble."

"I'll have to think about that to work it out.

"One last question. Where are all these photos from? They're all the same angle."

"A camera in the lobby of the hotel we use. Our clients sit and wait for their escorts and one of the boys secretly takes a photo. Only for a one-off mug shot. Blackmail would be bad for business."

They looked at each other.

"You're looking well, Tony. Retirement by the sea suits you."

"Thanks Mimi."

"Don't ever come back here. Forget Frankie. Make something up. Tell the villagers that he was found dead in a cheap brothel or something. Don't come back."

"I really don't intend to visit London ever again let alone your business. No offence."

"I know"

"Being the boss suits you Mimi."

"Thank you. Fancy dinner tonight? You staying here that long?"

"No thanks. I appreciate the offer but I really want to get back."

"I get it."

She watched him leave. Tony walked away and observed all around him until he got to the tube station and, even then, only let his guard down a little. He looked at everyone around him on the tube. No Butch or Maxi. He got out his iPhone opened the IMDB app and looked up Elvis's movies. 1967 Double Trouble. Shit. The character he played was called Guy Lambert. He had opened up another can of worms. He would have to confront Lambert and Sir Galahad when he got back to Rosegarden.

Chapter 33

Captain Nightingale allowed himself an extra half an hour in bed. It had been a busy couple of days and he had trouble sleeping, wondering about Scott and the knitting needles. Could it have been a murder weapon? Could Scott be a killer? He needed to speak to Tony about all this.

Daisy shook herself and then stretched and made her way up the bed to give the Captain a lick on his face.

"Good morning, Daisy. I know, I know, you want breakfast and a pee and a walk too. Come on then." He lifted her down off the bed, opened his curtains and looked out the window. The sky was like a blue and white slab of marble which could go either way later on, sunny or overcast. "Let's hope it's no too bad a day, Daisy."

He fed Daisy and let her out the back garden while he showered and got dressed then the two of them set out for Rosegarden.

When they got to the crime scene it was clean and pristine with out anything to note, as if nothing had happened, albeit Frankie Flake's van was now in Tony's garage.

Daisy ran down the ramp then slowed to do some zig zag sniffing. The Captain scoured the area for dropped food, the usual reason for this behaviour.

"I can't see anything, Daisy. Why are you acting like this? Come on, we need to get to Tony. Daisy. Come on."

She started walking towards the Captain with a look around every now and then at the interesting area. "Hm. We'll come back this way and see what interests you so. Come on now. Good girl."

It was nice to have a peaceful, undisturbed walk in to the village after the last few mornings. The sun was starting to win the fight against the clouds with more blue than light grey making up the sky. He noticed a few early tourists milling around the village before being able to check in to their hotels and B&Bs. It looked like the start to a great Easter weekend. Who knows what the result would have been if police cars, crime tape and detectives had been all over the place.

"Morning, Captain. Morning, Daisy."

"Ah, good morning, Michael. Nice morning for a run, eh? I see you like to keep fit."

"Yeah, working in the restaurant, it's easy to put on weight. Look at Paul. He loves to eat but never exercises. He's as wide as he's tall. A regular Mr six by six."

The Captain laughed. "Tony is quite fit as well."

"Yeah he doesn't eat much though. Fruit for breakfast and a meal at night. Maybe the odd fish and chips now and then. If he does that he doesn't eat much at night."

"I was about to see him. Is he at his flat or the restaurant?"

"Neither. He's on his way to London with Emma May. They left about fifteen minutes ago"

"Blast. OK it can wait until tonight I suppose. I won't keep you from your run any longer. Got to work off the pasta, eh?"

"You know it Cap. So long. You too, Daisy."

Damn, the Captain thought. "Oh well Daisy, shall we go tot the tea room for some breakfast?"

Daisy wagged her tail in consent and off they went, the Captain stopping and talking to people as they met and Daisy sniffing at plants, posts, walls and other dogs. The ten minute walk to the Cream Team took forty. "Can't wait for a toasted teacake and a pot of tea. A nice bowl of water and biscuit for you, old girl."

Maggie wasn't there when they arrived but Pearl and Jade served them with smiles and made a fuss over Daisy.

"No Maggie today girls?"

"She was in but she popped out to talk to Scott I think. Probably something about knitting."

"Ah yes, I've heard about the knitting circle. I'm surprised Scott knits to be honest. He never said."

"I know. He never talks about it. He is good though. I got my dad one of his fisherman's jumpers for Christmas. He wears it all the time."

"Is that so?"

Pearl left the Captain to have his teacake and tea.

"There's nothing we can do right now, Daisy. Let's Just enjoy the day."

He turned and looked at the calm sea and the sail boats and occasional windsurfers that glided upon it and the seagulls that danced around and forever laughed or cried or screamed or sang. It was the kind of day he and his wife loved to share. Walking along the promenade hand in hand. They were still new to Rosegarden then but people always stopped and said hello. They would get an ice cream from Frankie's predecessor. A happy old man with a sunny smile and a tale for every occasion. How different to how Frankie was.

His gaze drifted to the other end of the bay and the point that he cruised around with tourists pretending to look for pirates. He had only been in the smugglers cave once and found nothing. He had hoped to find kegs of rum and always wondered what it would have tasted like. Would it have been like the smooth and beautiful tasting rum you could buy in the shops for a premium. Would it have been as nice as Dom Papa or Kirk and Sweeney that the Seaview stocked? Probably not.

"How about we go to the Seaview on the way home, Daisy? Good girl"

Daisy had wagged her tail and the Captain took that as an agreement.

He wiped the crumbs away from his mouth and beard and called Daisy and they went out in to the warm April day. A distant argument grew louder from the end of the building as they neared it and the Captain hung back to listen.

"So where is it now?"

"I have no idea. I used the bullet that was on the beach as a rouse. I was on my hands and knees when Tony came out to me."

"It was such a stupid idea. A knitting needle of all things."

"Stainless steel and thick with a pointed end."

"I still say it was silly to give it to him. It killed him. If someone finds it they won't have to dig too much to know it was yours."

"It wasn't mine. I bought it for him"

"Yes but you bought it. After months or years of nobody caring to buy a pair of stainless steel knitting needles, you bought them."

"Well I couldn't find it. Maybe nobody else will either. I pushed it all the way in to the sand. It's covered"

"Let's hope so. But what about the other one? What did you do with it?"

"It's with all my others."

"Oh for Christ's sake, for a policeman you're pretty stupid."

"Maggie, after all we've been through together, this is not going to come between us, is it?."

"No. No it won't. Nor will it come between us and Ross."

There was a pause. The Captain wanted to see what what's happening. Radio would have to do instead of television, he thought.

"Please tell me you've told him."

"Of course. We don't have any secrets"

"Then why the hangdog expression?"

"Ross was so blasé about Frankie's death"

"You don't think he had anything to do with it do you?"

"No. I just wish he had more compassion. He has enough passion for both of us, but only I seem to have compassion."

"I'm glad you do, or else I wouldn't be here.

The Captain turned around and dragged Daisy with him silently and made his was back along the promenade. After he had gone as far as he thought he needed to he looked around. Maggie was going back into her tearoom. Charlie was nowhere in sight. "Come on Daisy. I need to have a Dom Papa in the Seaview lobby and think this through because at this moment, I'm very confused."

They crossed the road and the Captain turned around again. Charlie was on the promenade near The Cream Team, watching him. The Captain gave his usual hearty wave. Scott slowly waved back.

"Oh dear, Daisy. This may be a two Dom Papa visit to the Seaview lobby.

Chapter 34

Emma May was sitting on the bonnet of the Mustang waiting for him. She could tell straight away that Tony had a troubled mind no matter how much he tried to hide it. His smile and wave was that of someone putting on a brave face.

"Well don't you look gorgeous wearing a Mustang. Is this a calendar shoot or something?"

"Tony Martini, you will make me blush."

"Good, you look sweet when you blush. Let's stop at the services and have something to eat, you can show me your purchases too."

They drove off and, after a few miles of looking around and in the wing mirrors, he started to feel more relaxed.

"I'm guessing London was intense."

"I'll talk about it after we've had a bite and after you've shown me your purchases. If that's OK."

"Yes, of course."

He could sense his tension had transferred to her.

"Tell me about your day. Of course, leaving out the shopping part until the haul."

He smiled and put his hand on her thigh. She smiled and put her hand on his.

"Well, the shopping was the main part. I had a nice pot of tea and a lemon cookie in the main antique mall I visited. I bought an extra one for you."

"Ah, thank you."

"You're welcome. Anyway, there were two dealers at the next table talking about a friend of their's. One of the dealers saw this friend pull up to a car boot sale with his car rammed full of goods. Apparently, he said to this friend, 'you've got a lot in there today, Jimmy, but what's the rope hanging out your windows for?' 'Oh shit', Jimmy replied, 'I had an armchair strapped to the roof when I left home this morning'".

Tony laughed loudly, and so did Emma. "I didn't think I'd laugh as loud telling that as I did hearing it."
Tony laughed and told her how much better she made him feel. She squeezed his hand and kissed it and talked to let him carry on feeling better.
After they filled up with petrol and a services meal they went back to the car park so that Emma could do a haul of goodies.
"First off we have the biggest Stiltstons I have ever seen. Twenty one inches! Just had to buy it from an old tool vendor at a vintage shop."
"That's the biggest spanner wrench type thing I've ever seen."
"Like I said, it's called Stiltstons."
"OK" Tony laughed.
"Next I saw this shirt in a charity shop and had to buy it for you. Not Shaheen but a beautiful design and an Hawaiian label."
"Sweet of you, thank you. That's a great design and label. Ui Maikai. I think I have a Ui Maikai. Look at the beautiful embroidered label." He kissed her softly and she smiled just as softly and showed him a few more bits of clothes and a couple of books including a Haynes mechanics manual for an Austin Maxi. "Because you never know what your next repair job might be."
As the Mustang roared home, Tony told Emma some of what had happened.
"So this Mimi bitch from your past turns up. Jesus, that's a horrible coincidence"
"Yes it's not nice but, as far as the coincidence goes, it's been over ten years since I last saw her and if you go down this path you're going to bump in to the likes of her sooner or later. The difference now is she's the boss and there are two goons with her.
"The weird coincidence part is that at least two people from the village have had dealings with her."
"What?"
"I recognised one from a photo board she has, some kind of rogues gallery. The other she named, well, in a round about way. She kept

calling him Double Trouble. She then tells me, as I'm about to leave, that it's based on Elvis's character from one of his lesser movies."

"I only know a handful. Blue Hawaii of course."

"Of course."

"So who are they?"

"I want to confront them and make sure before I let everyone know."

"You know I can look up the Elvis clue."

"Yes. But I was hoping you wouldn't."

"I won't."

"Promise?"

"Promise. As long as you do a classic, 'I've gathered you all here', thing."

"I was going to do that on Monday evening. Let Easter happen without interruption. I have to ask a few people a few questions anyway, to get the whole thing straight."

Tony's phone sounded out a text alert.

"That was Paul texting for the Captain. Can you drop me at the Seaview when we get back."

"Of course. Something wrong?"

"I hope not."

Chapter 35

On Thursday Tony woke up alone, showered and dressed and went to his Hawaiian paradise rooftop terrace. Most of Rosegarden still slept and he looked around at the sunrise that was now at the height of its colourful stage and then looked back to see which of the houses reflected orange and then towards May's Garage where Emma slept in the flat above and he imagined waking up next to her as he had done the previous morning and smelling her hair and the touch of her skin against his and he couldn't wait to see her again.

He had a lot to do before he could do that. The Captain had told him all about Scott and Maggie and Ross and the knitting needle. It had taken a moment to get it straight in his head, but Scott and Ross had kept their relationship a secret. Tony wondered why. This was Rosegarden. Nobody cared about sexuality. At least not the residents. The tourists seemed to be open minded too.

But Maggie. What was the Maggie relationship. If it weren't for Scott, Maggie wouldn't be there? That's what the Captain had overheard. Why? The person who could tell him was Guy Lambert. Guy had a say on who came in to Rosegarden as a resident.

There were so many questions to ask before he found all this out. Perhaps one set of questions would answer the others.

Then there was Guy Lambert's set of questions. Was he Double Trouble? It did't seem likely. But there were so many secrets coming out it wouldn't surprise him.

He made a pot of coffee and grabbed a croissant and sat down at the table he had first heard about Frankie's death. It seemed like a month or more ago. If only Guy Lambert had agreed to the police coming in. The Captain couldn't ask any more questions. Poor Captain. He had done so much for the investigation and loved it. Then Scott gave him a look that had scared him. Or he thought he had. It would have been difficult to see an expression from that distance. Scott's wave was probably that of a man with a lot on his mind He had just had a grilling from Maggie. Whatever. The Captain was on his third rum when Tony got to him. Still outwardly chatty and Mr Social, but something showed through the facade. A sudden sense of age, maybe. Possibly a new feeling of vulnerability. He would probably be himself again today, but while frightened and nearly three double rums in, it showed.

A seagull circled and gave a lonely cry in the hope of an answer but none came. So it called out again and again until, eventually, another seagull, somewhere in the distance, echoed the cry. Then it flew in the opposite direction.

Chapter 36

He hadn't drunk that much at the Seaview but it had put him in the mood for rum and he had a couple of glasses of the strong rum Reno had given him at home then slept for twelve hours straight. When he woke he looked around for Daisy. She must have slept well too, for there she lay, on her back with her front paws held up to her chest looking for all the world like a snoring otter.

The Captain was an old hand at drinking. A large glass of water before bed alleviated most of his hangover, and after coffee, a couple of hot cross buns, and a shower he was ready to face a new day.

As he put on his deck shoes in the hallway there was a knock on the door.

"Good morning, Captain and Daisy."

"Morning Tony" The Captain bellowed like he hadn't seen him for months.

Daisy got excited and did laps of the hallway, lounge and kitchen.

"She's excited to see me."

"I'm glad to see you too, Tony. I wasn't so drunk that I don't remember what I said yesterday, I know that, but was it coherent and logical?"

"Perfectly, Captain"

"Thank God."

"Yes. I just wanted to ask if there was anything else that happened yesterday. I also came for a little more help."

"Well, nothing except what I told you. The conversation between Scott and Maggie. Then the look and knowing hand wave."

"Captain, I don't doubt you heard what you heard. However, how could you tell what Scott's facial expression was from that far? Could the wave be that of a man with a lot on his mind?"

"I see what you mean, Tony. You may have something there. I think the drama of it all may have taken hold of me."

Daisy jumped up on the sofa where Tony was now seated, opposite the Captain who sat in his throne of an armchair. Tony scratched her behind the ear and Daisy nuzzled in next to him.

"I have a friend for life here. She's so cute."

"Yes and she knows it. You said something about me helping you. I'd love to help more. What can I do? Who would you like me to follow or snoop on?"

"Oh nothing like that Captain. You've done your bit and provided a lot of very good information. No, this is desk duty I'm afraid."

"Well that's a little disappointing but I could probably do with a rest. What have you in mind?"

Tony pulled out a note book and camera from a brown paper bag. Daisy cocked her head with the rustling then laid out to sleep when she realised no food was involved.

"Oh so that's why Tony is flavour of the month. You thought he had food."

"Sorry, Daisy."

Tony handed the book and camera over to the Captain.

"So Captain, here are Frankie's notebook and camera. I've already found out some important information from it, but I wonder if you could have a look as well. There are times when he started and finished and left the van for any reason. There are also totals for ice creams sold and money taken. But he's also written a load of nonsense in the pages as well. Jumbled letters that don't make sense. I wondered if you could have a look and possibly decipher it all."

"I'd love to. Puzzles are one of my little pleasures. What about the camera?"

"Well, the battery is dead and I don't have a charger and I remember you and your late wife liked to take photos. I wondered if you had anything to charge the battery with or maybe take out the card and see what's on it."

"Yes we did. It was more Rosemary's hobby than mine. I liked the old days of film photography. She brought me up to scratch with the digital. I have her laptop and camera things stowed away. I'll get them out and have a look for you."

"Thank you, Captain. Who knows the killer may be on that card or in the book."

Chapter 37

Tony felt better knowing that the Captan was alright and felt useful as well.

Scott couldn't be the killer, could he? He would talk to him later after his meeting with Guy.

Guy hadn't seemed nervous or anxious or awkward. Tony told him about his trip to Executive Services to see what his reaction would be. It was blank. Totally over his head. Executive Services could have been a take-away for all he knew. That was on a FaceTime call though. He would get more from his body language when they spoke in person.

The tourists were increasing now, but, thanks to the limitations of accommodation and parking, it was never overwhelming. He recognised some regulars who greeted him and promised to dine at his restaurant at least once this weekend.

The meeting place was a bench overlooking the car park at the other end of the village. Not many used it. There was no great view and it was shady most of the day. Lighting a cigar he sat down and closed his eyes and began to think of all that had happened and how far they still were from catching a killer.

"Tony, old boy, not asleep are we?"

Guy Lambert beamed down at him. Everything was perfect, like he had just been unwrapped from a box.

"I wouldn't mind, to be honest, Guy. It's been a bit full on and not our usual sleepy small village pace."

"No, quite. So, tell me what you've dug up so far."

Guy simultaneously adjusted his cravat, pulled up the knees of his chinos and sat down next to Tony.

"I've found out a lot about all sorts but nothing that points to our killer."

"Go on."

"Firstly, Frankie felt the need to put on a persona for the people of Rosegarden. A totally different person to what the neighbouring farmers saw."

"Why? Why would he do that?"

"I think it's Charlie's influence. Have you been in Charlie's shop recently?"

"Erm, well, no. Not recently. I don't like people to think I'm overseeing everything they do or lay down rules on how they do business. What do they call that? Micromanaging?" Guy fiddled with his cravat.

"They won't think that. They'll think you're taking an interest."

"Are you saying I don't? That's really not true."

"I'm sure you do take an interest in your own way but people need to see that. In Charlie's case he needs a talking to. Or even closing down. He's turning it in to some seedy Blackpool novelty shop crossed with a soft porn shop.

"The swine." Guy paused for a moment "You're right, as usual, Tony. Hard to face up to thing's like that or even realise they're happening until someone gives you a sharp nudge in the ribs."

"Anyway, we'll get on to him in a moment."

"OK. What else is there?"

"I mentioned Executive Services to you earlier. Are you sure you don't know anything about it?"

After a few seconds of thought he shook his head. "No. Not a thing. I racked my brain earlier but nothing came."

Guy was cool and calm and didn't twitch or touch his cravat. Tony believed him.

"Why?"

"Because the two heavies who came here worked for that company. Albeit a one woman company. Unfortunately I know the woman. When you walk in a sewer shit will stick or at least the stench will."

"Right." Guy was trying to figure a link.

"At least three people with a connection to Rosegarden have had dealings with Executive Services. Frankie and someone calling himself Guy Lambert are two."

"What? The absolute shit! What swine would dare do that."

"We'll that's the second time you've said swine and I think both times refer to the same person."

"Blackpool porn shop or not. He's out."

Guy fuddled with his cravat and checked his blazer for fluff and returned to Tony.

"You said three people. Who's the other."

"Sir Galahad."

"Who?"

"I'll let go of that in a moment, but first, Maggie, Scott and your cousin Ross. Tell me about them."

Guy checked his cravat and then the pocket square in his blazer.

"What about them?"

"Maggie was overheard telling Scott that if it weren't for him she wouldn't be here. You have the final say about who comes to live here. What was her story."

"Ross and Scott brought her to my attention. She had a business that was doing well until her business partner left her and took a lot of the money with him. They had met her and visited her cafe when it was thriving. They went back several times and then one day she was getting ready to sell it to a loan shark she was indebted to. They suggest she start a cafe in Rosegarden and here we are. She took over the Cream Team when Agnes died. She's done a brilliant job and is good for the village."

"I like Maggie, you don't have to sell her to me. That is interesting, though. So is the fact that Ross and Scott hide their relationship. This is Rosegarden. It was founded on inclusivity before that was a word. 'Equality and Respect for all' is the motto and even an idiot like Charlie knows that."

"Yes but you have to respect not just a person's sexuality or identity but how they want to portray themselves. Joan and Paula are openly gay and so are Dr Jo and Beth and they are all very open about it. Roy Greening, on the other hand, is gay and everyone knows it but he never mentions it, has never had a partner and never promotes the Pride Festival. That's his choice. Scott and Ross want to keep their relationship secret. For their reasons, which I don't know. So be it."

"That's fair enough."

Guy considered Tony for a moment.

"So who is Galahad?"

"Sergeant Scott Hayward."

Chapter 38

"Damn it, Daisy. I haven't arranged the weekend's boat trips yet."
Daisy stopped licking her paw and looked at the Captain.
"Don't worry, old girl, we'll go out for a walk in to the country today."
The trips were booked from the Seaview Hotel, so the Captain's first call was to find out numbers.
"Fully booked on all three days? Excellent. Thank you."
He looked at Frankie's notebook and camera lying on the coffee table. "That will have to wait, eh Daisy? Let's have a picnic this afternoon and I'll go through the book then. The camera will be tonight's entertainment."
The Captain spent the next two hours on the phone. The smugglers were all set to pose in front of the cave. Hattie was OK to do the ornithology section. Tony agreed to two of his staff helping and if all else failed, he and Emma would do at least one day on the boat serving refreshments and doing basic seaman jobs. He even said they would do the Friday and, if they liked it enough, the Sunday too.
"All settled. OK, old girl, time to make a picnic and get ready for a long walk."
They set out half an hour later with plenty of food and drink for both. The Captain walked as if his heavy rucksack wasn't there and smiled to himself. "Plenty of life in the old boy yet, eh Daisy?"
Daisy wagged her tail and headed to the beach. "Daisy, no. Come on, this way." She looked back at him then reluctantly trotted back.
"We'll go to the beach later. Now for grass and wild flowers and maybe the odd, stray cow for you to bark at."
They walked for an hour before settling for a flat piece of land at the top of a hill that overlooked the bay and Rosegarden in the distance, so that the houses merged into one white and sage green shape with a multi coloured top. Behind them, he could see fields and farmlands and, way in the distance the tops of occasional cars

and lorries that were too far away to hear. He took out his binoculars and looked out to sea and then to Rosegarden. He couldn't make out faces but saw a few cars pull in to the East car park. There were more spaces there now that Frankie's van was absent.

"Let's forget all about that horrid business while we eat." He poured out some food and water for Daisy, took out his sandwiches and a flask of coffee and slowly ate and took in the view. The breeze blew inshore to cool down the sun which, by now, was warm and on it's initial decent towards the sea. The ambient and hushed sounds of nature were the only things he could hear. Waves murmured distantly and even the seagulls seemed to be taking a rest.

"It's good to be alive, Daisy, even if you miss the ones who aren't."
She gave him a cocked head look and then walked away from her empty food bowl to sniff the countryside. He finished off the last bit of sandwich and lay back to watch the few small clouds that dare venture out in the sun. I'll look at the notebook tonight, he thought and closed his eyes.

*

The Captain woke up with something licking his face. "OK, Daisy, ok." He opened his eyes and saw a cow looking down at him.

"Oh my God. What's happened?" He looked to see how low the sun had gone then checked his watch. Only half an hour had passed.

"Daisy. Where are you Daisy?" Standing up he noticed a few cows had gathered around him, slowly chewing the cud and grazing. Other than the face licker, none took any notice of him. "Daisy." His call was louder and more worried. "Where are you?"

There was still no sign of her. He grabbed his binoculars and scoured the countryside form where he stood. Nothing. This was the hilltop and he had a view of the surrounding area. She wasn't that fast so she couldn't have gone too far in half an hour. Maybe she ran after a rabbit. Oh God, she was half Dachshund. What if she had tried to burrow in to a hole?

"Daisy." His shout was louder and higher pitched than before. Still no sign of her. He pointed the binoculars towards the beach and the sea and the village. "You little rascal. What are you doing all the way down there." The little figure of Daisy was on the beach, rolling in the sand and then zigzagging around. "Bad girl."

Walking down the hillside would have been tricky at speed and would have taken a while. Walking down to the road and along it was safer but would take a little longer. All he could hope was a passing car would stop for him. It did ten minutes in to his walk back he heard a horn. It was Molly in her beat up old land rover.

"Hey Cap. Want a lift? Where's Daisy?"

"Yes please. Daisy is the reason I need a lift, the little devil"

"Oh dear. Where are we going? In to the village."

"Just to the sand dunes near my house please. She's made her way to the beach. I fell asleep and when I woke up she was gone. Put me in a hell of a panic. Spotted the little rascal with my beanos."

"Oh, that must have been horrible."

The Captain looked across at Molly's smile and felt a little better.

They got to Lookout Point and Molly tooted her horn as she took off.

"Right, Madam. No treats for you tonight." he said out loud climbing to the top of the dune to looked around. There she was, sniffing for all she was worth. That same area as before. This time she stopped and circled. She's going to roll, thought the Captain. Oh no, what is she going to roll in. But she didn't. She started scratching at the surface then digging. By the time the Captain got there she had exposed a ten millimetre, stainless steel knitting needle. The Captain pulled it out the sand with his hankie and looked at the end. It was covered in dried blood.

Chapter 39

The Crow's Nest was never busy in the daytime. Because of it's location at the end of the eastern peninsula, which jutted out to sea further than the one in the west, people began turning up there an hour before sunset to watch the spectacular colours that shone out all over the bay and reflected off the white buildings of Rosegarden.

It was the polar opposite of the

Fisherman's Arms. Although over two hundred years older, it always looked newer, more stylish and chic than it's rival. It only served light meals in the evenings and was more of a Bistro or Wine Bar.

When Tony sat there waiting for Scott, he was the only one in the place. He had briefly asked the management, Scott and Liz Corey, about Frankie but knew they wouldn't have anything new. They didn't buy ice cream and Frankie didn't drink wine or eat bistro food.

Tony was early. He planned it that way so he could choose the table and his seat with his back to the corner walls and a clear view of the door.

Scott walked in and, after adjusting to the lower light level, waved hello at Tony who smiled and nodded. "I bought you a lime and soda. That's your tipple on duty isn't it? Got myself one too. I can see why you drink it."

"Thanks, Tony. You didn't have to."

"That's alright. Come and sit opposite . We have a lot to talk about."

"Oh you've made progress in the case?"

"You could say that."

Scott took off his helmet and placed it on the table next to them.

Tony let him get settled.

"Alright. First things first. I went to London, as you know, and followed up on the license plate number of that car."

There was no change to Scott's face.

"Have you heard of Executive Services before?"

"No, can't say I have." Scott looked interested and sipped on his drink.

"Oh wait a minute. That was one of the cards we found in Frankie's room."

"Apart from that, are you sure you haven't heard of them?"

"Quite sure. I don't understand what you're getting at or asking me, Tony."

"Well, I'd only heard of them through that card as well. Turns out that the person who runs it knows me from my unpleasant past. A lady by the name of Mimi. She's something of a modern day Madame. Runs escorts out of that swanky office in London. I suppose she has called her business many things in the past. To keep it fresh and dodge the law."

Scott was nodding but still looked nonplussed. "Keep going"

"Anyway, at some point and with another company name, she got a photo of a client she called Galahad. A knight in shining armour who saved a poor woman from the very evil clutches of Mimi and her organisation."

Scott turned pale.

"Do I need to go on, Scott? Or should I say Galahad?"

"I.."

"Take a drink and compose yourself and tell me all about it. I'm guessing the woman you saved was Maggie. Am I right?"

Scott nodded and took a drink then bowed his head and didn't look up.

"Scott, remember I'm a friend. I doubt you've done anything wrong."

"I've kept secrets and lied to people."

"I bet you did that for altruistic reasons, not for self gain."

Scott met Tony's eyes.

"I've found out about you and Ross. I respect that you want that to be kept secret but, if that is why you're finding it difficult to find the words, I already know."

After a pause to give himself time to think, Scott started.

"Ross and I go to London every now and then. Not often, maybe three times a year in the off season. On one such trip we saw Maggie coming in to our hotel. We had met her a couple of times before in the tea shop she used to have in the countryside outside London. She tried to sneak past us but we said hello and tried to have a conversation. She awkwardly took her leave and went to her room. We talked about knocking on her room door but then saw her go back to the lobby and wait for a while then went back upstairs with a man."

Scott took a drink.

"Later in the evening we saw her do the same but with a different man. She looked so out of place. I can't explain it but it was like her smile was false and she acted like she was grateful to each man for meeting her.

We decided to be nosey and snoop. The same thing happened three times that night. We couldn't believe it. When we thought she had retired for the evening we knocked on her door. She looked petrified. She was expecting her minder to turn up and she thought we'd all be in danger. Ross, being a hothead, wanted to stay and have a fistfight with the minder but Maggie assured us he wouldn't be using his fists. She gave us a business card for the agency and told us to ask for Gail. Don't ask why they gave her that name, it's disgusting."

Tony stopped himself from telling him he knew why. Both men paused for a drink. "Would you like something stronger, Scott?"

"Yes, please. Bourbon please."

Tony got up and got the drinks.

"Two bourbons"

"Thank you."

"No problem, I wanted one too.

"So what happened when you phoned the agency?"

Scott let the taste and sweet burn fill his mouth. "That's a good quality bourbon."

"When you drink spirits, it pays to buy the good stuff. Now please, continue."

"I phoned and asked for Gail at the latest appointment possible. It was so cold and straightforward, like I was booking an appointment with a hygienist. I was told to wait in the lobby in the same seat that we had seen the other men wait. Gail came down and took me to her room. Ten minutes later Ross knocked and came in and Maggie told us how she had been trapped in to prostitution. Her business partner in the cafe had run off with all the money and she paid bills and got on top of things using a loan shark. She couldn't go to the banks because the partner had emptied the accounts and left debts there too. Before too long she couldn't pay it off and the loan shark took the business and told her the only way to pay off the debt was to work for a friend of his. It all spiralled and before long she's meeting clients in a hotel lobby."

"So how did you help her escape?"

"Well we didn't have a lot of time before the hour was up. We took Maggie to our room and Ross stayed with her. I went in to the lobby and just outside the door, I messaged them when the minder made his way to the lift. I ran up the stairs. We were staying on the third floor and Maggie's room was on the sixth so they had time to make their way down and we made an escape as soon as I knocked on our door. We got on the tube at the nearest station and headed to Waterloo and got the first train we could, as far as possible. The night was spent talking, the only people in the provincial train station. I don't even remember where it was. The next day we made our way here. Maggie stayed with Ross who gave his cousin the abridged version of her sad tale, leaving out the part about prostitution."

The two men sat in silence for a while. Tony finished his bourbon and said to Scott "I'm going to ask this because I have to. In my head I already have the answer. Did you kill Frankie?"

"Good God, Tony. No. Of course not. I gave him something to protect himself from whoever he was afraid of. Besides, what has this got to do with me, Maggie, Ross or any of that other business?"

"Scott, slow down. I don't think you killed him. I just had to ask. It may have nothing to do with the three of you or maybe the two who came from London were after you. I have my suspicions about who got in contact with them. I can't figure out why so many people from our sweet village got caught up in Mimi's seedy world."

"Who else?"

"Well Frankie and somebody Mimi referred to as Double Trouble. To get to the end of a long story, someone used the name Guy Lambert while they paid for services from Mimi."

"Who?"

"My guess is Charlie. I need you to fingerprint something for me."

"What?"

"The murder weapon you gave Frankie to protect himself with."

Tony reached down to the seat next to him and produced a blood tipped, stainless steel, 10mm knitting needle and put it on the table between them. For the second time Scott turned pale.

"I need another bourbon."

Chapter 40

Captain Nightingale was glad of the peace and quiet. His windows were open and the sea could just about be heard along with Daisy's snores which came from the other end of his sofa. He thought it was the sweetest sound and one that gave comfort and a feeling that nothing bad could happen, no matter how many times it did.

Tony had been amazed with his find. Daisy's find really. He said he was meeting with Scott later that afternoon. That would have been an awkward and miserable time. The murder weapon had been found. What they could prove with that was anyone's guess. Did Scott kill Frankie? Tony doubted that. So did the Captain.

Oh well, back to the book. What did all this mean. Reading the letters it was easy to see that Frankie had the intellect of a child. He was easy to take advantage of and acted out of stupidity more than malice or a need to be shocking. If the wrong person had asked Frankie to jump off a cliff he probably would have.

OK so what do these symbols mean? + - x Maybe they relate to the letters next to them. Frankie wasn't smart enough to figure out a code, as such. Is it a code? "What do you think Daisy?" He said out loud.

Daisy raised her head slightly. She was very tired after her escapades. The Captain couldn't stay angry with her. Especially after finding the murder weapon. She was a funny thing. Always wagged her tail at certain people and acted aloof with others no matter how happy they were to see her.

He looked through the book again. "I think I may know how to work this out Daisy, and it's thanks to you."

It's starting to make sense. The last day he was alive it says:

TM x - -	PM + + +	DF - + +
PA - - +	RA + - -	RG x x x
JD x x x	JJ - - -	MC - + +
BB + + +	SH - x +	CO x +

"Daisy, if you met someone you liked you would wag your tail. If you met someone you were indifferent to, you'd be aloof. On the rare occasion when you dislike someone you'd growl or bark. I think these notes are Frankie's equivalent. It's not a code, it's a shorthand diary. He met with Tony. He doesn't like him, Tony's indifferent to him. What's the third one? The outcome? HM, how will we know without asking everyone." He gave it some thought.

"I know. When did he start off slightly miserable but ended up laughing when you ran around the sand like a loony? Last Wednesday."

He found last Wednesday's entry. There it was CND - + +.

"Yes. Indifferent, we were happy and at the end so was he."

He looked through some more. People he knew Frankie liked and disliked. The code, or shorthand, worked. He looked again at the last day. "There was no outcome with CO. Or maybe Frankie wasn't around to write it."

Charlie Osborne the murderer? He was a vile buffoon of a man, but capable of murder? Who knew?

It was time to look at the contents of the camera. The batteries were fully charged and a bright electronic musical noise sounded when the Captain switched it on. After a few fiddly attempts he managed to access the pictures stored on the card. They all seemed to be fairly innocuous, mainly at the beach from the ice cream van. "Oh that's a good one of you, Daisy" he said out loud. Daisy just changed position and rolled on her back doing her best otter impression. He noticed the image number, displayed on the bottom, said 10/560. "This is going to be a long process, Daisy. I think I need to look at them on the laptop." It hadn't been turned on since Rosemary went in to hospital. He plugged it in to the charger, powered it on and the MacBook chime sounded, followed by a pause, then a photo of their wedding day as the desktop picture. He had forgotten it was on there. He closed it up and went outside for some air. He picked up a couple of tissues on the way back in to wipe away his tears and Daisy was waiting for him. She stretched up on her hind legs to be lifted up and licked his face when he did so. "I'm OK old girl. I just wasn't expecting to see that."

He put her down and she followed him to the desk and lay down on his feet while he opened up the laptop to see Rosemary smiling and happy. "I miss her, Daisy. But I can't be sad when I remember how much happiness we shared. I know, how about some music. Let's see what I can find on here."

He opened up Music and found a playlist called 'Favourites' and started the tunes playing. He smiled as Neil Young's Harvest Moon, started, remembering all the impromptu dances it triggered. "OK trawling session resumes here."

It was quicker and easier to look through the images on the laptop using the left and right keys to go backwards or forwards. As before, nothing stuck out as alarming or important or full of clues. Just various people, mainly women, as seen from the ice cream van and none were that rude. They could have been shot by an amateur photo journalist doing apiece about the seaside. After about fifty photos he came to the end of that folder. He hadn't expected that. Then he realised it was the most recent. Somehow the laptop had split up the photos in to folders. On to the next. These were totally different. Mainly taken at the back of Caught in a Dream, behind the plastic strip curtain. These were all of women bending over. The next folder showed various women from various angles and all seemed intrusive, like images from the mind of a peeping Tom.

The next were all women posing naked. The Captain looked away as if to shield innocent eyes, then looked again but this time at the backgrounds. They all seemed like they were taken in a hotel room. Folder after folder were the same. Some were more graphic. All the women were submissive. Were these all taken by Frankie? He was going to look to see if he could tell when they were taken and go from there but he didn't need to. The last photo in that folder was taken in a hotel room but this one had a mirrored wardrobe. There, reflected in the glass was the chubby naked body of Charlie Osborne.

Chapter 41

Tony, Captain Nightingale, Scott and Guy met at Guy's house for a debrief and update before the Bank Holiday weekend got under way.

Tony was the spokesperson for the group and laid out the findings so far giving details of all the investigations and those involved.

"So to summarise," Guy began, "Frankie was easily persuaded and led by Charlie Osborne. Most, if not all, the perverted and less than savoury behaviour has its origins in Osborne's mind. We think Osborne was putting pressure on Frankie to do his will but Frankie was getting tired of the whole thing. This is from what the people you spoke to have said and also the contents of the camera. The photos Frankie took were less intrusive and graphic than those we can credit to Charlie based on the times of the metadata. At this point Osborne threatened him with telling this Mimi and her thugs about Frankie. For some reason, we think he carried out this threat and on Sunday night the thugs came looking for him. They were too late because Frankie had already been murdered with the thick, stainless steel knitting needle that Scott had given him to defend himself. What we don't know, or at least what nobody has told me, is who killed Frankie Flake? Any ideas?"

"Well, my money is on Charlie." Said the Captain. "If my decoding of his diary is correct, then Osborne was the last person to see Frankie alive and there was no third entry after his initials."

"That's if they were his initials, Captain. There are other people in the village with those initials."

Everyone looked around at each other. "I can't think of any, Guy"

"Really, Tony? How about Chloe Oliver?"

"From your hotel? Going from everything we've heard and what Chloe said, Frankie would have put plus signs for everything. Sorry, Guy, that doesn't fit. The only other CO I know is my niece Connie Occhino and I know that's out the question. She was busy all Sunday, she had no motive, and if she had time to go to Frankie's van, there would have been plus signs all the way."

"Ok, ok, I'll concede Charlie looks good."

"Also, all the messages and emails from the iPad and iPhone were sent when Frankie was at his van. The only person with the passwords and codes was Charlie."

"Yes, yes, Scott, I agree with that, but have we got any proof? Hard evidence? The smoking knitting needle, as it were?"

"No but I have a plan."

"Please don't tell us you're going to plant evidence, Tony."

"No, but Charlie won't know there were no usable fingerprints on the weapon. We'll confront him with the weapon and tell him we can link it to him and trap him that way."

"Hm. It may work but it may not. Anyway, from now until Monday evening at the meeting, nobody is to discuss this any further with anyone. No investigations, no questions, no trips to London. It is to be a normal, wonderful, Rosegarden Easter weekend. I phoned Charlie and acted as if I knew nothing about the state his shop is in. I also led him to believe that nobody knows anything about the murder but we're going to have a next steps meeting on Monday evening. By then Dr Jo should have the autopsy results and I'll make a final judgement about how or if to tell the County Police."

"With great power comes great responsibility, eh Guy?"

"Yes, Captain. It does."

Chapter 42

Frankie was forgotten. At least over the Easter weekend. Tony and Emma joined the Captain on his Friday boat trip and Emma did Saturday and Sunday too. The Captain liked her choice of music. Not something he had thought of before, but Emma's playlist of Northern Soul and chilled jazz was just right. On Sunday Tony joined them again and worked as sailor and barman and spent as much time as possible with Emma.

The restaurants were full at lunchtime and through the evenings. The tourists made their choices over The Crows Nest or the Fisherman's Arms and some tried both, and couldn't choose which they liked best. The shops did a good trade apart from Caught In A Dream. Charlie only sold a few tea towels and a box of fudge. Nobody wanted his novelties and went elsewhere. Luckily, Guy Lambert had placed an urgent order and collected some goods himself. He placed the stock in various shops and they soon sold.

The beach displayed its blue flag and Connie did a roaring trade in soft serve ice cream. Only a few complained that there was no scoop ice cream available, but were soon won over by Connie and her generous servings.

The Gutty Shark had a manageable queue and Ollie amazed the customers by remembering what they ordered on their previous visit last year. The Cream Team was busy and Pearl and Ruby had no time for chatting or leaning and Maggie made sure everything was as it should be in her realm. All the international restaurants delighted the visitors with their tasty dishes and Tony's mind was kept away from the body in his garage.

Even the Ling brothers had to work simultaneously cutting hair and giving shaves and their Tai Chi lessons filled the beach in the evenings.

Everyone was busy and everyone was happy and the seagulls laughed along with the fun times and all the time Frankie lay momentarily forgotten in the chiller in Tony's garage. Soon though, it would speak volumes to Doctor Joe who, by Sunday evening, was driving back home with Beth and trying to remember everything she learned about performing a post mortem.

Chapter 43

Tony wondered how many other people woke up early on a Bank Holiday Monday to help with an autopsy. He stared down at Frankie. "That's where the Easter weekend ends." He said to Paul and Mike. They nodded in bleary eyed consent.

"When do we move him to the table, Tony?"

"Wait for Doctor Jo to turn up. Oh, here she is now."

Doctor Jo swept in through the large garage door with her leather doctor's bag that had been a congratulations present from her mother when she got the practice at Rosegarden, almost twenty years ago.

"OK, where's the stiff?"

Paul and Mike stepped to one side to reveal Frankie in the chiller.

"Oh my God, he looks like a sample in a jar. Poor bastard."

"That's what we said, right Mike?"

"Right."

"I'm guessing this old food preparation table is where I'm to perform the autopsy."

"It's the best we could do. Is it big enough?"

"Yes, Tony. It's fine. OK let's load him on here."

The four of them pulled him out of the chiller and hoisted him on the table.

"OK, Jo, what can we do to help?"

"You studied the crimes scene, so you can answer any questions I have. Maybe Mike can hand me tools and Paul can take notes."

They got settled and Dr Jo began.

"OK from the head down. Paul if you could mark on the diagram that there is a bump to the back of the head the size of a walnut. There is no bruising around it or signs of it being recent. Next thing to note, there is a recent bruise and indent on the front of the head about two and a half centimetres, or one inch if you prefer, above the left eyebrow. Tony?"

"Yes there was a little blood on the edge of the counter that could have caused it."

"Ok. Good. Also to note is a bruise on the right cheek. There is a little blood in the nose. Tony?"

"There was a lot of melted ice cream on the floor and it had even got beneath him around the edges. I couldn't see any blood on the floor but my initial guess was that the bruise and blood was from the fall."

"Yes, possibly but there is no real way of knowing."

After a pause and a drink of water, she continued. "Going down, I can't see any signs of a struggle. No bruising or scratches to the face or neck. Nothing to the top of the torso. Looking at his fingernails, oh, there are none. He's chewed them way down. OK let's have a look at this hole in the chest."

From her bag she brought out a pack of, what looked like, long cotton buds, took a mouthful of water and then put the tip of one of these in her mouth. "OK, let's measure the depth." She stuck the moistened tip in to the hole and then drew it back out, and took a measurement with an old wooden ruler.

"You get a lot in that bag, Dr Jo."

"Yes, Tony. Mother bought me this when I got the job here. She wanted it back when I came out."

Tony laughed. "I'm glad you stuck to your guns."

"Always. Anyway, the depth of the hole is approximately three and a half centimetres. So enough to pierce the heart. But this just missed the heart. If he had been stabbed outside his van and stumbled around he may have been able to get to a hospital in time to save himself. It's hard to know exactly. But, if it happened how you think it happened, he was stabbed, fell forward, hit his head and was unconscious when, or just after, he landed, then he may have bled to death. Was there a lot of blood?"

"It didn't seem so. The ice cream obscured everything but it was more pink than red. If he had bled to death, surely it would have been redder?"

"Probably. Anyway, let's continue." Dr Jo looked closely over the rest of the front of the body. "Ok let's flip him over."

Dr Jo studied the back of Frankie's corpse. There was nothing to note until she got down to his calves. Out of the bag she pulled a large magnifying glass. She pushed a button on the side and a strong light light was emitted. After studying an area of the left calf for a few minutes she asked Tony, "were there any insects in the van?"

"Insects?" Tony thought about it. "A couple of flies and a wasp."

"Ok. For now it looks like the cause of death was bleeding to death from the hole in the chest. I'll run some tests and, possibly, be more conclusive later today."

She paused and took out a scalpel from her bag.

"Now comes the fun part. Do you have any scales?"

"Scales? Only in our kitchen no old ones around here I'm afraid."

"OK. Can you get me some food bags then."

Tony looked puzzled.

"I need to weigh some of the organs, I'll need to take them to the surgery and I'm not putting them in my bag. No matter what I think of my mother."

Tony sent Mike to get some and then watched Jo work with the scalpel.

"You should be a chef. That's great work."

"Thanks, Paul, but you have now put me off going anywhere near Tony's restaurant."

Once the organs were bagged she snapped off her gloves and said, "I should have a report for you later this afternoon before the meeting."

"Thanks, Jo."

"Bank holiday Monday, my arse."

Chapter 44

Tony and Emma sat on the roof top paradise having breakfast and watching the sky darken until the drizzle started.

"That really is the end of the Easter weekend."

"Not really, we're still off today and together."

"True. Come inside and I'll show you my record collection."

"I bet you say that to all the girls."

"No, only the gorgeous ones who drive Mustangs."

Tony poured coffee while Emma flicked through his LPs. There were a few Hawaiian and Exotica albums that went with the rooftop decor, some Elvis, of course. The jazz ones got her interested and she chose Miles Davis' Kind of Blue. Some blues in there and soul. "You have a Bobby Bland. I love Bobby."

"You found the soul section then?"

"I took out Miles already but Bobby might have to be first."

Tony put the record on and joined Emma on the sofa.

"Fancy just quietly reading for a while and enjoying the sound of the rain and Bobby and just chilling?"

"Sounds good to me."

They settled in and let the ambience envelop them. Emma was reading an Agatha Christie she found in Tony's bookshelves and Tony settled for a magazine then got distracted by Frankie's notebook which he had got back from the Captain on Sunday. It had been on the coffee table ever since. He flicked through it.

"Did you go to Frankie for ice cream last Thursday?"

Emma put her book down after finishing the paragraph she was reading. "Erm. Yes, that's right. After work."

"How did he seem?"

"I thought the questions were over?"

"They are. I'm just testing the Captain's theory."

"OK. When I got there he was sad. I was happy and when I left he was happy too."

"Bingo. The Cap is right."

He turned to Sunday's entry. Something puzzled him. "That's weird."

"What?" Emma put her book down again. Tony didn't notice she was getting annoyed.

"Chrissy mentioned she bought ice cream from Frankie on Sunday but there's no entry for her."

"Chrissy? Old man Hawkins granddaughter?"

"Yes, she said she went to Frankie's on Sundays and some evening's. There's not one entry for her."

"What initials are you looking up?"

"CH. Chrissy Hawkins"

"Chrissy's mum married Richard Howells."

"Still, it would be CH."

He thought about their interview with her. "Oh shit. We need to go to Hawkins farm and talk to Chrissy."

"So much for a chilled Bank Holiday Monday."

Chapter 45

The drizzle turned to rain by early afternoon and afternoon turned to evening without anyone noticing. The umbrellas, drip drying by the meeting room door, grew in number until all the committee were accounted for. They took up their favourite seats in the easy chairs and sofas that informally faced Guy Lambert, Tony and Dr Jo.

"Good evening, everybody. Thank you all for coming out in this weather. As you're all probably aware, this isn't a normal committee meeting. Following the discovery of Frankie Flake's corpse on Monday, investigations have been carried out by Tony and Sergeant Hayward along with some help from Captain Nightingale. Also, Dr Jo has carried out a post-mortem today and will tell us of her findings. But first I'll hand you over to Tony."

"Thanks, Guy."

"I've gathered you all, here. Haha"

Everyone looked around at Charlie Osborne who sat chuckling away at his own remark.

"You won't have much to laugh at by the end of this, Charlie."

"I haven't done anything. I didn't kill him."

"Are you sure about that. Are any of us confident that we didn't have some small part in his death?"

The room stirred and mumbles grew until Bill Fisher asked "What do you mean? We didn't kill him."

"I didn't say anybody here killed him. I said we all had a small part to play. I know I did. If I'd taken more time to find out about him things may have been different. If Guy had taken more of an active role in finding out about everyone. If we had all been more welcoming to him he may not have sought out the only familiar and apparently friendly face he knew, Charlie Osborne."

The room shuffled and looked at Charlie.

"What? I was the only friendly face. You lot never gave a shit about him. You all thought he was perverted and creepy."

"Thankfully a few people in the village and all the surrounding farmers thought differently. If they hadn't, we wouldn't have found out how much you controlled and manipulated him. He was your shield to lead a sleazy life. He was your way of distracting everyone's gaze. Unfortunately for you, Charlie, people saw through it. They saw the other side of Frankie. The many sides of Frankie. Most people only see your sleazy side. The side that filled Caught In A Dream with sleazy tat. How did your shop do this weekend, by the way? Not too good I hear."

Charlie shuffled and squirmed. The room did the same.

"So let's see what happened to Frankie. Last year I saw him with his iPhone. I thought he was scrolling and browsing the internet. Like the rest of the village, I believed he was a pervert or something. But it wasn't his phone, was it, Charlie. He was making notes for you on how much he had sold. You were skimming of the top of his sales. He worked for me. That's my money. We can talk about that later. Between sales he was snapping women in their bikinis. Again for you, on your phone. He never knew the passwords. You were always coming over and pretending he had forgotten them. When I banned the phone from his van, he kept a diary of sales. He turned it into a personal diary. I'm guessing you used that for skimming the money off him. When did you set him up with a second hand iPhone and iPad?"

Charlie shuffled and said nothing. The room was intrigued and kept looking over at Charlie.

"Danny Fisher is an expert on all things tech and he had a look through the iPad and iPhone we found in Frankie's room. Apart from setting up face recognition and fingerprint ID, it's doubtful he ever looked at them. There was almost nothing on them. Only a few things to point him out as someone who continually looked at porn and escort sites. Which he never did. The times those were accessed were times he was in his van selling ice cream. You slipped up Charlie. Firstly. you left your fingerprints on those devices and nobody else, apart from me and Scott, touched them until Danny investigated them. Secondly you sneaked in to my staff's lodgings uninvited to set Frankie up. You did it when he wasn't there and couldn't possibly have used the iPhone or iPad."

"I never killed him though."

"No, but you probably played the biggest role in his death."

He paused and looked around the faces in the room who looked back in disbelief. Then he looked at Charlie again.

"If you hadn't contacted the escort agency in London and told them to come down here, none of this would have happened. Why did you do it?"

Charlie seemed to be trying to think of the words but all he came out with was. "I was hoping they'd just beat him up and scare him."

"Why"

"He was pissing me off and not playing along anymore. He had messed things up in London earlier this year and he promised he'd make it up. He didn't. I wanted shot of him. I didn't think they would kill him though. I just wanted to scare him."

"You scared him alright. He went around everywhere looking for weapons to defend himself with. He ended up with a stainless steel knitting needle provided by Sergeant Hayward". Tony looked at Scott.

"Yes, I provided him with the knitting needle. I realise it was daft. But I thought if fighting got close, at least he'd have something. I thought about giving him a kitchen knife but I just thought he'd probably hurt himself more than anyone else."

"But we still don't know who did it. Who killed Frankie Flake?"

"OK Ron, I will tell you who stuck the needle in him, but I can tell you it wasn't a fatal wound."

Tony looked around and paused, and took a drink of water. This had been a struggle. He was alright making a toast or putting on a show for his customers now and then, but this had been a lot. It was a lot of heavy as well. Time to finish it off.

"Because of everything you have heard so far and because of Frankie's notebook, or diary, which had also been mentioned, we believed that the last entry, CO, referred to Charlie Osborne. We therefore thought he was the killer."

"Piss off. I didn't kill anyone."

"We know. We know we were wrong on two counts. Firstly, CO referred to Chrissy Howells. Chrissy drops her aitches. Frankie thought her name was Owls and called her a real hoot. It was a joke they had. When Chrissy went to see Frankie he showed her the knitting needle. He told her it was a rubbish weapon and would never protect him against anyone. Well, after a lot of debate, Frankie convinced Chrissy that even if she gave it a good thrust it wouldn't even go through his coat. He was wrong of course. Chrissy panicked and pulled out the needle and ran, throwing it over the van and on to the beach. Frankie collapsed and bashed his head on the counter and lay face down, bleeding."

"She didn't come to us sooner? That speaks volumes." Roy Greening looking around for agreement. Nobody looked back at him."

"Because we were pretending that Frankie had run off, Chrissy thought he was still alive. She was worried all Sunday night, and frightened too. Then our 'group lie' got out and she relaxed and was even happy for Frankie. We questioned her again and asked if she had seen any blood around the van and was Frankie hurt. She broke down and told us."

"So did Chrissy kill him indirectly? Like manslaughter. Poor Frankie. Poor Chrissy, she's just a child really."

"Cassandra, Chrissy still believes the lie and I'm not going to tell her different. I left her at Captain Nightingale's with Emma and Daisy. She's getting dog therapy right now."

"But somebody has to be accountable for the man's death." A couple of people murmured agreement with Ron.

"If Frankie could have got help straight away he probably would have survived. Of itself it wasn't a fatal wound and even if he had come round when he should have he still would have been alright. I think Dr Jo better explain the rest."

"Hello everyone. Well I really did come back to a shit show didn't I?"

A couple giggled, the rest of the room looked down at their feet.

"Well, going by what Tony tells me of the crime scene and my autopsy I would suggest that the sequence of events and cause of death were as follows. Though I would like to point out that I'm no pathologist."

She paused and looked around the room.

"The first thing was the knitting needle in the chest. Yes it was the right size and weight and it was sharp enough to do damage. Going by Chrissy's build and weight, I would say that Frankie either leaned forward on impact to prove a point or he may have slipped on ice cream that had been dropped on the floor. The engine would still have been running for another hour and the ice cream would not have melted by then. Back to the wounds and what they tell us. There was some bruising and a little blood around the face. It is my guess this happened when Frankie collapsed from the wound and a, hit his forehead on the counter and b, hit the floor of the van. According to Tony, the ice cream that coated the floor by the time the body was found was more pink than red. This suggests that there was less blood than ice cream. I do not believe that Frankie bled to death. After weighing the vital organs, I would also suggest that none failed before death. What I do believe to be the cause of death, from my autopsy and Tony's observations, is a violent allergic reaction to a wasp sting which caused a fatal heart attack. I tested Frankie for this sort of allergy and the results point to this as the most likely cause of death."

The room murmured then erupted.

"A wasp sting?"

"A bloody wasp?"

"You mean to tell me that I have been made miserable and maligned and all this time it was a wasp sting. I'm going to see a lawyer about this whole thing."

"Oh shut up Charlie. You deserved all you got. If it weren't for you, he wouldn't have been scared out his wits and that knitting needle would still be unsold in Rosegarden Hardware. As someone pointed out to us, Frankie fitted in and had more right to be in this village than you."

"How do you know anything about it, Sergeant plod? If it weren't for that oily wop doing all your work for you, you'd still be figuring out what to do."

"That's enough everybody. Now quiet."

Everyone did as Guy told them.

"Right. It's my fault it got as bad as this. I'm glad we found out all the sordid things about you, Charlie. I want you out by the end of April, by the way. Don't care where you go, but from the first of May you are barred for life from Rosegarden."

Guy visibly calmed himself.

"OK, as I said, I take responsibility for this whole sham. If I had called in the police from the start it would have been over before Good Friday. Having said that I have decided.."

As happened on the meeting on Monday, Guy was interrupted mid sentence by the door flying open. But this time it wasn't the Captain.

"Well hello, everybody. The drunk publican told me I'd find Guy Lambert here."

"What? Who are you? What do you want? I don't know you madame."

"Oh, so this is the real Guy Lambert. I thought that chubby pink thing, sinking further down in his easy chair, didn't fit the name. Mr 'Tall Dark and Handsome In an Old Fashioned Way" suits the name much more. So what's his name?" She said pointing to Charlie with her chin.

"Charlie Osborne."

Anyway, why don't you introduce me to your friends, Tony."

"Guy, everyone, this is Mimi."

Chapter 46

Captain Nightingale watched the wind hit the window and the raindrops race each other down to the frame.
"You can stay here as late as you like, Chrissy. If you need to phone your parents, let them know that Emma is here also. If they need you to go home she can drive you in her Mustang. Is that OK, Emma?"
"Of course."
Chrissy went in to the hall way to use her phone.
"Poor girl has been through a lot"
"Yes, Emma. I thought we all had until now. I agree with Tony. Frankie is alive and on the run."
Daisy snored against Emma's leg. She had fallen asleep there, tired and worn out from all the affection.
The Captain went to the window and looked out at the rain. In the distance, away from the village, a car's full beam lit up the side of the hill. The lights were getting closer. Strange that someone should drive into Rosegarden on a Bank holiday evening. Everything's shut and the hotel and B&Bs weren't checking anyone in until Wednesday.
Chrissy came back in to the room. "They said I should stay until the rain dies down or for a couple of hours. Whichever's soonest."
"Well let's get comfortable. The Captain doesn't have a TV but we could play music and a game or something. How about a hot chocolate?"
"Yes, please."
"Would you like to show me where everything is, Captain?"
He continued to stare out the window.
"Captain?"
"Sorry, what?"
"Would you show me where everything is to make a hot chocolate?"
The street outside lit up. The Captain turned to the window.

"Sorry, ladies, not now.

"Chrissy, help yourself to anything. Wait for us to come back. Tony and Emma will take you home, later."

"What's the matter? Where are we going?"

"The car from London just went past. Let's get to the meeting, fast."

Chapter 47

Butch and Maxi took position at opposite ends of the room, guns drawn.

"I want to see everyone's faces please."

Everyone looked around or twisted themselves to be face on.

"My God. Look at you all. It's like a reunion from different phases of my career. Tony from my bad bitch days. I'm not a good girl now but you should have seen me then. Right, Tony?"

"You certainly had a well deserved rep."

"Then from my fledgling, post prison days we have Sir Galahad. What is your name Sergeant?"

"Scott Hayward. Does it make a difference?"

"Not really. Just wanted to put a real name to a face."

She looked at more faces.

"Oh my God. OMG. If it isn't the fair maiden Galahad saved. Gail. How are you? You looks so, what's the word? Dowdy? Frumpy? Matronly? Spinsterly? Anyway not like my top oral girl."

"Fuck me" Shouted Osborne.

"I doubt that. You liked women of colour. You called them Pakis and coons and chinkies, suffixed with the word birds. I'm guessing it made you feel superior for five minutes. They all reported back that your micro penis was anything but."

"My God, Osborne. You can start packing tomorrow. I'm not having you around here any longer."

Mimi took a silenced gun from her Gucci shoulder bag and shot Charlie Osborne. "No need for him to pack now."

Screams rang out and crying started.

"Oh quiet. All of you. Stop whimpering or I'll start with you lot instead of finishing with you."

The room quietened down to gentle sobs.

"There that's better."

"You came here to kill Charlie? Why?"

"We'll apart from the skin crawling vile things he has said and done, he paid me off in counterfeit money. Can you believe it? We frogmarched him to the bank and he got dodgy money out of his safety deposit box? He thought he got away with it too. Tried to get in our good books by ratting out his mate. We were never interested in Frankie. Just wanted to get Charlie's whereabouts out of him. Speaking of ratting out your mates, Tony, before I kill you, tell me truthfully, did you rat us out to the cops?"

Before Tony could answer the door crashed open and twenty one inch Stiltstons smashed in to Mimi's skull. Emma May stood in the doorway, wild eyed, teeth bared in a snarl and Mini's blood splattered up her face, ready to raise her weapon again. The Captain was behind her, wide eyed and trying to understand it all. Maxi raised his gun and aimed at her, Butch raised his gun and aimed at Tony. The pift noise of the silenced guns was followed by panicked screams and then everything was quiet except for a chorus of gentle sobbing.

Chapter 48

Tony found Emma kneeling down and firmly holding her makeshift weapon. "You saved my life twice. She was going to shoot me and then Butch was going to shoot me. Thank you isn't enough. I'm glad you bought that big spanner thing."

"Stiltstons, Tony. Stiltstons. Me too. You saved my life too . He was aiming for me."

"You moved but, yeah. In the end they shot each other."

"Wait a minute, did you say his name was Butch? Seriously?"

"Yeah. Anyway, we've got to move fast. First let's check on the others."

Everyone started moving slowly and standing as if expecting more horrors.

"Is everyone OK? It's over now people."

"Is anyone hurt? Does anyone need treatment."

"I think a few could do with a sedative, Jo. Where's Guy?"

"Guy? Where are you?"

"He's lying over there."

"Thanks, Emma. Damn, I wish I bought my smelling salts. Yes I still do have some. He's out but seems OK."

Tony looked around. Four dead bodies. The survivors held each other. Scott and Maggie. Mama Cassandra, Bill Fisher and Ron Greening held hands. All were in a state of shock and seemed trying hard to understand it all. Everyone looked towards a groan that came from the doorway. The Captain was starting to move and sit up.

"Captain. Are you OK. Were you shot?"

"I'm fine. I think Emma got me on her back swing when she hit that thug."

"Sorry, Cap."

"I'm ok. Nothing a Dom Papa wouldn't fix. So what now Tony?"

Everyone looked at Tony. He had to think quickly. They'd have to phone the police this time.

"OK everyone, listen to me. I know you're all shocked and saddened and confused but we're going to have to think clearly now for the sake of the village. We need to phone the police."

Guy Lambert had regained consciousness and was being held up by Dr Jo. "Quite right. Should have done it the first time."

"Yes, Guy. But that's in the past and we need to think about now and the next few days. First off we need to get our story straight. This is how it happened. Mimi and her goons were here looking for Frankie. We don't know where he is. She shot Charlie and said she would carry on shooting until we told her Frankie's whereabouts. At that point Frankie came in and whacked Mimi over the head with Stiltstons. Goon one shot at Frankie and hit Goon two. Frankie grabbed the gun and shot Goon one. He then dropped the gun and ran off with the Stiltstons."

"Oh crap."

"Yes, sorry, Emma. Unless you want to go to prison you're going to have to lose them."

"I don't know, Tony. Look where the last group lie got us."

"It's that or Chrissy and Emma go to prison, we all get charged with accomplice after the fact, Scott gets put in prison for tampering with evidence and Rosegarden is tarnished with a bad and unlawful rep for a long time to come."

"He's right, Guy"

"Yeah, Tony's right."

Guy looked around at the nodding faces.

"OK Tony what do we do."

"Well thankfully the guns had silencers on so nobody outside of this room heard anything.

"We'll need at least half an hour's head start. After I leave here, wait a full half hour, no, make it forty five minutes then phone the police. Mimi mentioned that she spoke to Steve at the Fisherman's and she asked about Guy Lambert. Captain you need to tell him to change his story. We need to get rid of Frankie's body. My guys will do that with the Captain's help."

Tony stopped for a moment and looked in Mimi's bag and pulled out cards and keys. "Bill, we'll need Danny to come with me and Emma to London."

"What? Now? Why?"

"We need his tech expertise so we can make sure nothing in Mimi's office links back here. If we go tomorrow the police will get there before us. That's why we need a head start. Let's just hope they're attending other crimes in the area."

Chapter 49

There were no other crimes that night. Not within a thirty mile radius anyway. Luckily, there was a delay in the police attending a multiple killing. They didn't believe Guy when he phoned them. Scott had to phone them back. There was a silence when they asked him why he didn't phone them first. He came up with the plausible excuse that he was securing the crime scene, although the real reason was that he didn't think of putting himself forward to phone and left it to the leader of the village. By the end of the second phone call an hour had passed, better than the requested forty five minutes. Another forty five minutes went by before, for the first time in its history, Rosegarden was filled with blue flashing lights reflecting off the white buildings, wet roads and rain soaked pavements.

People came out from all over the village and gathered under their umbrellas and discussed what could have happened.

By this time Frankie's old ice cream van had transported his dead body to the secret path, known only to the Captain, local historians and the amateur actors, that led to the smugglers' cave. The corpse had been placed inside the unplugged freezer to keep any insects or wildlife away from it. The freezer only just squeezed in to the van, thanks to the fact that Mike and Paul had started stripping out all the shelves and cupboards during the past week. One side was done which made the van lean heavily to one side with the weight of the freezer.

Frankie was in his makeshift tomb at the back of the cave, finally resting in peace and away from the indignity of being squeezed in the chiller. His last function was to wrap his hands around the Stiltstons and grip one of the guns. Tony helped him out with that and then took the weapons back to the crime scene.

He then had a three hour drive with Emma and Danny back to London. Tony and Danny commuted in from West Ruislip where Emma waited for them. Congestion charges, CCTV, Number plate recognition; all would put a car from Rosegarden in the vicinity of the offices of someone who had been killed in Rosegarden. There could be no trace. Tony even took the precaution of everyone leaving their phones at home. They had Charlie's iPhone and iPad, that he had pretended were Frankie's. Emma followed Tony's movements via the 'Find My iPhone' function on the iPad.

They made their way in to Central London, looking for all the world like a father and son on a night out. They both wore dark, unbranded clothes and put up umbrellas against the rain that had just started falling there. They were as anonymous as a pair of headlights and soon found their way to Executive Services.

The key fob from Mimi's bag didn't work on the pad at the front of the building and there was no obvious lock. They went round the back which was now abandoned. At the doorway where he met Butch, Tony tried another fob lock and the door opened after a few beeps.

"Alright, gloves on, Danny."

They worked quietly, Tony looking for any paper files or photos and taking down Scott's photo from the board. He looked at the board again and took down Detective Superintendent Cooper's photo. Another connection to him. He searched all the other offices and rooms and found nothing.

"How's it going? Did you get in?"

"I did but it will take a lot of hours to go through all this. We just don't have the time. I can look through most of the cloud files quickly. There aren't many there?"

"Why do you reckon she did that?"

"You can get rid of a physical hard drive quickly and without any records. But, even if you delete something from a cloud based system, there's no guarantee it won't be kept somewhere. The police probably have enough experts to dig into that."

"OK, quickly look through what you can in the next half hour, then remove the hard drive and I'll search for USB sticks."

"There's one on that bunch of keys. If we're lucky she didn't keep anything on her phone. She seemed careful so I doubt if she did."

"Yeah, let's hope Butch and Max did't keep diaries."

Danny laughed and started trawling files. Tony found five USB sticks dotted around and did a second sweep and found three more taped under desks, one in a fridge and one amongst the teabags. A third sweep produced nothing. Danny found nothing of interest on the cloud. Tony gave the photo board another look and took down all the photos.

They made the last Tube and got back to Emma with a hard drive, USB sticks and three burner phones that Tony found in a small storage cupboard next to the back door as well as a bunch of photos.

Halfway home, on a dark road away from CCTV, they threw the iPhone and iPad out the window into a field. They were wiped of prints and all information.

"Is that it now, Tony?"

"No, we have to dispose of Frankie's body and all this stuff. But don't worry I have a plan."

"I bet you do."

Chapter 50

In their long illustrious career, it was the first time the County Police left a serious crime scene smiling. They weren't smiling at the four bloody corpses or the forensics that had been carried out or the smell of cordite that still lingered. They weren't even smiling because they could call it a day and go back home to a hot shower, pyjamas and bed. They were smiling at the hospitality shown. All the cups of tea, hot chocolate and coffee as well as the packs of biscuits that circulated, were just the start. After Maggie had been interviewed she opened up her cafe and dragged Ruby and Pearl away from taking selfies by the blue lights, police cars and ambulances to help serve the police who were given free drinks, cakes and sandwiches with apologies for them not being as fresh as she would normally serve.

Even stern faced Detective Ken Jordan cracked a smile. It was an easy crime scene that matched everyone's accounts. They had a criminal on the run and had alerted other forces that he was dangerous and, although all the weapons were accounted for, may be armed. In the morning he would contact the Met in London to find out anything about this Mimi and her henchmen. They had their phones so the tech guys would search those too. It was an easy case. Not open and shut; this Francis Fennelli, aka Frankie Flake had to be found and questioned. It would probably take months, maybe years. Nobody knew a thing about him. Just a seasonal worker who didn't mix with anyone.

That idiot Sergeant should have phoned straight away. This Frankie Flake could be anywhere by now. It may be time to replace him. That would be for others to decide.

He gave the signal and messaged for everyone to pack up and go home for now. They may have further questions down the line, though probably not.

Chapter 51

By the time the village started coming to life the rain had stopped and left a chill in the air. Most people slept late and by the time everyone was awake the sun was shining and yesterday's rain began to evaporate.

Those who didn't know what went on the previous night wanted to know and those who did know wanted to tell them, but Guy Lambert was to address everybody in the Village Hall at seven that evening.

At quarter to seven the Village Hall was almost full and a only few stragglers got there with minutes to spare. Everyone in the village had shown up by the time Guy took to the stage and stood behind the lectern.

"Good evening, everybody. As you are all aware, for the first time in its history, Rosegarden saw blue flashing lights of both the police and ambulances. Some of you may have seen body bags being loaded in to the ambulances."

There was a collective sharp intake of breath and quiet murmuring.

"I know how frightening that is for us all. Another first in the village's history happened last night. A group of three villains found their way into our beautiful village, entered this building and got inside the main meeting room where they held the committee at gunpoint."

More sharp intakes of breath and excited whispers chorused in response to Guy Lambert's call.

"They were after Frankie Flake. A man who not many people knew. Then again very few people tried to get to know him, myself included. From what we have discovered, Frankie wasn't the bad person some of us thought he was. In fact the opposite is true. He was a person unsure of himself, shy, complex, unable to communicate very well and a man who was easily influenced. Unfortunately, the Frankie we all saw was influenced by the wrong type of person. But that person was the only person he knew when he came here to work. The only person who seemed welcoming."

Guy looked around at the crowd who now seemed a little uncomfortable.

"When did we veer from the path my grandfather set out? His vision, his foundation for creating this village was what became our motto. 'Equality and Freedom For All'. I'm sure if the first Guy Lambert was here he would have gotten to know Frankie before everybody else. Before Frankie could be influenced by others. If he had seen that Frankie wasn't being true to himself he would have given him the freedom to be himself and treated him equally. We took Frankie on face value and saw the wrong face."

The village were now nodding sadly as one.

"What happened last night was people with evil intent saw the wrong face of Frankie and wanted to punish him. I don't know where Frankie has been this last week but he turned up last night and saved all but one of the committee from being killed. The one person from the committee who was killed by the criminals will go unnamed but I will say that he was the bad influence on Frankie."

The village nodded and murmured the name that Guy wouldn't speak.

"As for the criminals, Frankie killed one with a large spanner."

Emma restrained herself from shouting "Stiltstons"

"The other two criminals killed each other thanks to the quick actions of Emma May and Tony Martini"

There was applause and happy murmurs.

"Frankie fled to avoid arrest. Although we are all law abiding citizens, I do hope it is a long time before he is caught."

The village laughed and murmured agreement.

"We will need to sort out a few details in terms of shops and so forth but these will be relayed to the village as soon as we have ironed out the details."

God, that's another cliche I hate, thought Guy Lambert and the village rose and chatted and went home.

Chapter 52

The Mustang Rose hummed quietly along in the moonlight. Captain Nightingale tried to think why he hadn't thought of moonlight trips before. Possibly because they would have been too late in the evenings in June and July. He'd put it to Guy when it was convenient. It was far from convenient at that moment. He was with Tony, Paul, Mike and Scott and Frankie. Frankie was in his specially designed casket heading out to the deepest part of the bay.

Tony and Paul were drilling small holes through the lid of the freezer which encased Frankie's corpse. The lid was screwed down and inside were all the electronics and photos from Mimi's office, and the few effects that Frankie left behind. If a maritime Archaeologist dug the freezer up in the future they would think Frankie was a highly regarded king with a wealth of gadgetry. They may have been puzzled by the old anchor placed at the bottom of the freezer which was also drilled full of holes.

The engine stopped and they drifted a few feet while the Captain lowered his anchor.

Each man grabbed a piece of strapping and hoisted the freezer on to the side of the boat and then let go to see it disappear in to the deep blackness of the sea. Looking around at each other, they caught their breaths and no-one spoke until they were nearing the dock. "Nothing will be the same for a while, but we need to pretend it is until then."

They nodded their heads in agreement with Tony.

Epilogue

After Charlie Osborne's funeral it was announced that Scott would take over Caught In A Dream, which was to be renamed Rosegarden Souvenirs. It was agreed to partition off a third of so that Danny could run a new technology store and repair centre.

Scott enclosed a resignation letter with his final report from Rosegarden and recommended that a police presence was not necessary in the village. The County Police agreed but let Rosegarden keep the Morris Minor. Emma gave it a service and a re-spray and the village used it to transport people to Rose Park.

Bill Fisher replaced Danny with Jimmy Ling which pleased the rest of the village.

The village settled back to their tranquility and everybody turned up for a double wedding; Scott and Ross's and Dr Jo and Beth's, performed by Guy at the Place of Worship.

Tony and Emma's Shaheen collections grew but they remained living apart and spending nights at each other's apartments.

The Captain began moonlight cruises and even took Daisy along.

Where Frankie's ice cream van once parked there is a plaque which reads,
"You never really understand a person until you consider things from their point of view.. Harper Lee"

Printed in Great Britain
by Amazon